"Step away from your mother, young Pamina," the Lord Sarastro said. "I will not ask again. Instead, I will compel."

❧

And so, I stepped away, pulling my hood down over my face, for I had begun to weep in earnest and did not want to give my father and those who did his bidding the satisfaction of seeing me cry. The second I stepped away from my mother, I could feel the wind begin to rise. Tugging on my cloak with desperate, grasping fingers. Howling like a soul in hell.

Over the scream of the wind, I heard my father shouting orders in a furious voice. Then I was gripped by strong arms, lifted from my feet, and thrown like a sack of potatoes over someone's shoulder.

The last thing I saw was the flame of my father's torch, tossing like some wild thing caught in a trap.

The last thing I heard, dancing across the surface of the wind like the moon on water, was a high, sweet call of bells.

❧

"Once Upon a Time . . ." is timely again in these retold fairy tales:

THE STORYTELLER'S DAUGHTER
by Cameron Dokey

BEAUTY SLEEP
by Cameron Dokey

SNOW
by Tracy Lynn

MIDNIGHT PEARLS
by Debbie Viguié

SCARLET MOON
by Debbie Viguié

SUNLIGHT AND SHADOW
by Cameron Dokey

From Simon Pulse
Published by Simon & Schuster

Sunlight and Shadow

Cameron Dokey

SIMON PULSE
New York London Toronto Sydney

First Simon Pulse edition July 2004

SIMON PULSE
An imprint of Simon & Schuster
Children's Publishing Division
1230 Avenue of the Americas
New York, NY 10020

Designed by Debra Sfetsios
The text of this book was set in Adobe Jenson.

Printed in the United States of America
2 4 6 8 10 9 7 5 3 1

Library of Congress Control Number 2004100041
ISBN 0-689-86999-1

For Amanda, who was there for the finish
For Lisa, who was there at the start
For Jodi, who was there for everything in between and then some
And for Hilary, who gave me my first glimpse of the
Queen of the Night

A House Divided

Come close, and I will tell you a story.

Or, at the very least, I'll start one.

The story isn't mine alone, so I shouldn't be the only one to tell it. But, as I think it's only fair to say the whole thing started with my parents, it seems equally fair that I should be the one to get the storytelling ball rolling.

This is how the whole thing began, to the best of my knowledge.

In a time when the world was young, and the *hows* and *whys* of things you and I now take for granted were still being sorted out, Sarastro, Mage of the Day, wed Pamina, the Queen of the Night. And, in this way, the world was made complete, for light was joined to dark. For all time would they be bound together. Only the breaking of the world could tear them apart.

In other words, in the time in which my parents wed, there was no such thing as divorce.

I don't know how long they were married before I came along. How many days and nights went by. Of all the questions I asked as I grew, and I asked plenty, until I learned that questions didn't always equal answers, that particular question was one I never voiced. I think this is because I wasn't all that old before I figured out there was another way of asking the very same thing:

How long before all the trouble started?

Because trouble is precisely what I was.

Never mind that my appearance was inevitable, all but foreseen and foreordained before the cosmic ink on my parents' marriage certificate was dry. Sooner or later, I was bound to put in my appearance, and that meant that, sooner or later, a husband would have to be found for me. This caused friction between my parents while I was still an infant, drooling in my cradle.

I can tell what you're thinking:

That must have been uncomfortable.

Not drooling, a thing all infants do, but growing up knowing you are the primary source of tension between your parents, both of whom you would like very much to love. Since you've already been intelligent enough to come to this conclusion, I see no reason to deny it. Why begin my story with the telling of a falsehood?

You're absolutely right. It was.

Imagine you have ants crawling over your body, so many you can never quite brush them all off. No sooner do you relax, thinking, *I've finally done it this time!* than you feel a prickle and an itch in some body part you could have sworn you'd taken care of only moments before.

The sensation isn't horrible. Not exactly. It certainly isn't painful. These are only tiny black kitchen ants, not ants red with anger, ready at a moment's notice to sting and bite. The trouble is, the sensation never ends. Those ants are with you every single moment of your life. You never have an instant's peace, awake or asleep. For, when you lie down to rest, with no distractions, it sometimes feels as if the ants will smother you completely, flowing over your body like a great black tide.

That's what it feels like to live in a house divided.

Let me take a moment to describe it for you. I think it will help you to understand what I'm talking about. The house where I grew up, where my parents lived together, yet apart, is set into the top of a mountain, the tallest in any direction as far as the eye can see.

Actually, I suppose it would be more accurate to say that the house *is* the top of the mountain. Two great buttresses of stone and glass facing opposite directions, set back to back. Like a statue with its arms stretched open wide, each reaching for a prize unobtainable by the other.

My father's side of the house faced due east, the better for him to catch the very first rays of the morning sun. My mother's side faced west, the better to keep an eye on the rise of the moon and the onset of stars. And the mountain itself comprised the whole wide world, so that there was no part of creation in which my parents did not play some part. No place where creatures lived and breathed that did not know both light and dark.

This, of course, is just as it should be. It may even sound familiar. But I will say again that the world was a very different place when it was young. In that time, sunlight and shadow did not live in the world together in the same way that they do now. When the sun shone, its light bathed all the world. When it went down, darkness covered all.

And, as the years went by, people came to worship the one even as they came to fear the other. So that, even though my parents shared the world, they did not have an equal share of power, for the love of the world was most definitely lopsided. This had pretty much the effect you might expect. My parents first grew to resent, and then to distrust, and, finally, to fear one another.

They say that opposites attract. I've heard this. Haven't you? I don't know what you believe, but I think that it's true. The trouble is, between attraction and understanding there can be a very great distance. Too great for any one individual, no matter how strong and powerful, to cross on her or his own. It is a distance which must be crossed by both, together. How long this takes is not important. What matters is that the journey commence in the first place, that the parties involved move steadily toward one another until, at long last, each is safe in the other's outstretched arms.

As far as I can tell, my parents never even packed their bags, let alone set out. With the possible exception of me, they weren't all that interested in the things they might have in common. They were more interested in the things that kept them apart.

And so my mother never saw that the rising of the sun could be a thing of beauty. Never saw the way the color returns, first peering over the edge of the world, then tumbling over and over and over itself, like brightly dressed children turning somersaults.

And my father never took the time to see the beauty of the moonlight. Never noticed the way it caresses everything it touches with a sweet, white kiss, turning even the branches of dead trees into decoration as fine and lovely as mother-of-pearl inlay on an ebony box.

What he would have seen had he looked at me, I never knew, for he never saw me. Or, if he did, I never knew it. Due to an agreement made at my birth, the result of a cryptic and dire prophecy, I would not officially see my father until the day I turned sixteen. On that day, I would be considered of marriageable age and would move from my mother's side of the house to my father's, the better for him to select the proper husband for me.

Asking for my opinion about whom I might like

to spend the rest of my life with was not, apparently, considered an acceptable option.

And so, though he was only half a house away, for all intents and purposes, I grew up without a father. Though I did catch glimpses of him from time to time. Unlike my mother, unlike either of my parents, for that matter, I was not confined to the dark or to the light. I could move freely in either.

As I grew older, I began to make it my business to discover as much about my father as I could without him knowing about it. In this way, I learned that he never laughed, that his hair was dark chestnut flecked with gold, and that, when the weather turned chill, he wore a cloak of this exact same color. But it is difficult to learn much about someone when you can't let them see you.

I did learn one other thing, however. And that was that there lived in my father's household a girl who was almost exactly my age. One he was raising as if she, not I, were his daughter. She was tall and graceful, where I was merely tall and often awkward, and dark, where I was fair. And her eyes were as green as holly boughs.

She was the daughter of his forrester, my mother finally told me, though only after I had pestered her so often and for so many years I must have driven her almost out of her mind.

As a general rule, my mother refused to speak about my father. Her business was her business, and his was his. She could no more explain his actions than he hers. It did no good for me to ask *Who? What? Why?* and certainly not very often.

But, as my sixteenth birthday began to grow close, then closer still, my mother seemed to change her mind. The only conclusion I can draw is that it finally dawned on her that it would be in my best interest to have some understanding of my father's side of things, of which the dark-haired girl was clearly an important part. And so, she finally gave me the long-awaited, much-asked-for explanation.

She waited until almost the very last minute. She told me the night before my sixteenth birthday.

"Her name is Gayna," my mother said.

We were sitting in her observatory, my favorite room in our part of the house. The ceiling was all of glass and almost completely round, poking out from the side of the mountain like a great soap bubble. Sometimes, when I was younger and would awaken in the night, I would find my mother in this room, standing absolutely still with her eyes upon the stars, as if they held some message she had yet to decipher.

"Whose name?" I asked, a little sulkily.

We had both been on edge all day, knowing it might be our last together for who knew how long. My mother had arranged for dinner to be served in the observatory, a thing which was usually one of my favorite treats. Tonight, neither of us had eaten much.

"The girl you've pestered me about for time out of

mind," my mother replied. "The one who's always with your father."

At this, I sat bolt upright, my food altogether forgotten.

"Why?"

"Why what?" my mother asked with just the hint of a smile. "Why is she called Gayna? Why is she always with your father? Or why am I telling you this now?"

"I don't care what she's called," I said boldly, though we both knew I did care, very much. "And I can figure out why you're telling me now. It's because I turn sixteen tomorrow."

"That leaves the middle one, then," said my mother. "She resides with your father because she is an orphan. Her mother died giving birth. Her father was gored by a wild boar when she was five. There being no one else to raise her, Sarastro took her in."

"So," I said after a moment. "He will raise a stranger's child but not his own."

"Gayna's father was not a stranger," my mother said. "He was your father's forrester. This I have already told you."

"But *why?*" I burst out once more. "Why should he care for her and not for me? It isn't fair."

"No," said my mother. "Perhaps not. But it would be a mistake to think your father cares nothing for you, Mina. If anything, I fear he cares too much. Your marriage is the most important thing in the world to him. He sets great store by it."

At this, I could feel my understanding, to say nothing of my patience, stretch almost to the breaking point. This may seem somewhat precipitous to you. I'd ask you to remember I'd had fifteen long years filled with precious little information in which to try to figure all this out.

"My *marriage*," I echoed, and even I could hear the bitterness in my voice. "But not me, myself. How can he choose a husband for me when he doesn't even know who I am?"

"A just question," my mother agreed, her own voice calm. "And one I once posed myself. Now finish your dinner," she went on briskly as she rose from the table, and in this way, I knew the brief period of answering questions was over. "The hour grows late and I have work to do."

At her words, I felt a spurt of panic. *This may be the last night I hear her say this,* I thought. Tomorrow night, for all I knew, I would be having dinner with my father and the daughter of his forrester in some great hall filled with smoking torches. Some place where I could be pretty certain they did not welcome the night.

"May I not come with you?" I blurted out.

A smile touched my mother's marble features. "Of course you may," she replied. "Eat something while I fetch you a cloak with a nice big hood. If you're coming with me, that unfortunate hair simply must be covered up."

With that, she turned and left the room. I ate my

dinner as fast as I could, in a manner that wasn't at all ladylike.

I'll eat all my dinners this way from now on, I thought, suddenly inspired. *Then perhaps my father will be so appalled by my manners he'll give up on me entirely and send me back where I belong.*

This thought cheered me so much I took the biggest bite yet and dribbled gravy down my chin. Quickly I wiped it off. Who knew when I might spend time with my mother again? I didn't want to begin our last night together with a scolding.

"Hold still, now," my mother said as she returned with a cloak and a rosewood box full of hairpins. Black ones, of course. Swiftly she tucked and pinned every strand of my unfortunate bright hair up out of sight and tied a black scarf around it beneath the hood for good measure. Then, together, we went out into the night.

How shall I describe it to you? How shall I tell what it is like to move through the darkness with my mother at my side? She cannot be separated from the night, for she is its living embodiment. Her face, as pale as the moon when it is full. Her eyes, as silver as the stars. She has no need to bind up her hair, for it is as dark and lustrous as the sky at midnight. She is beautiful, my mother, and the great sadness of my childhood has always been that I look so little like her.

At least we have the same name, Pamina, though Mina is what I prefer, most often, to be called.

I don't mean that my mother rules the darkness.

She doesn't, not precisely. She doesn't make it come and go, for instance. The universe does that all on its own. It's more that she is the guardian of the night, of the things that belong to it. She keeps them safe and in their proper place, just as my father does for the things that belong to the daylight hours.

We walked in silence for quite some time before I realized where we were going: through the thickest part of the forest to where my father's favorite room looked out over his side of the top of the mountain. It was but a short journey, even on foot, a thing I always found surprising, showing, as I thought it did, that my parents were much closer than they cared to acknowledge. There, my mother stopped, her face turned up to where, almost at the mountain's top, a shaft of golden light stabbed out into the darkness.

"Do you see, Mina?" she said softly. "Do you see the way your father tries to impose his will? The way he will not accept, but seeks to defeat, the darkness?"

I did see, of course. But my mind, which even moments ago had spontaneously plotted ways to displease my father and so encourage him to return me to my mother, now leaped to his defense.

But what if he just wants to read a good book? What if he's come to the very best part and doesn't want to stop just because the daylight has gone? Must the lighting of a lamp always be considered a crime? Do we not pull the shades to keep out strong sunlight?

Of course I did not say these things aloud.

Instead I said, "Why did you ever marry in the first place?" A question to which I'd wanted the answer for as long as I could remember.

"Because it was necessary. It is still necessary," my mother replied after a moment. "There are some things which must be in order for the world to exist, Mina. The marriage between your father and me is one."

I bit down, hard, upon my tongue to keep from asking just one thing more, the thing which I had always wished to know the very most. It didn't do any good. I asked the question anyway. I'm just made that way, I suppose.

"But did you never love each other?"

My mother was silent, gazing up at the light streaming out from my father's room. Silent for so long I became all but certain she wouldn't answer at all. Then, just as I was beginning to feel altogether wretched, she said:

"Yes, we loved each other. Once. It might even be the case that we still do. It's been so long since I've thought of such things that I no longer know. But I do know your father and I have never understood one another. And without understanding—"

My mother broke off, her eyes still fixed on the light.

"Love is like water, Mina," she continued after a moment. "Water, in all its forms. It can squeeze between your fingers like your own tears. Burn and freeze your heart at the selfsame time. It can evaporate before your very eyes in no more than an instant.

Making a reservoir to hold your love is the most difficult task in all the world. You will never do it if you do not understand first yourself, and then your beloved.

"Have you heard the saying, *Still waters run deep?*"

"Of course I have," I said.

"But do you understand its meaning?" asked my mother. "It's the best way I know to describe abiding love. Remember that phrase when your father marches his parade of potential husbands before you. Look for the place within, the reservoir where love may reside until it fills to overflowing. Do not be dazzled by outside appearance, for that is merely what the sun does best: It shines."

"I will remember," I promised.

"Good," said my mother. Then she turned and laid her hand against my cheek. "Go inside now. Sleep, and have sweet dreams, my daughter. For tomorrow is a big day. You will be sixteen and I must take you to meet your father."

"Yes, but will you?" I asked, intending to tease, for my mother had never gone back on her word as far as I knew. Not to me, nor to any other. I knew that she would keep her part of the bargain made at my birth, no matter what it cost her.

She laughed, but the sound was without mirth.

"Now you sound just like your father. His greatest fear all these years has been that I'll change my mind at the very last minute, find some way to keep you all to myself."

"He doesn't know you very well, then," I remarked.

"On the contrary," a new voice said. "I know your mother very well."

With a cry, my mother spun around, thrusting me behind her. Not that it did any good. For, in the same instant, torches flared to life all around us. As if the very ground had opened up and spewed forth fire. And so, in the space of no more than a few heartbeats, we were surrounded by my father's soldiers.

I think my mother understood what he intended at once, though I wasn't far behind her. There could be but one cause for this. My father intended to take me away before the appointed time.

"No," my mother said, a statement, not a plea. "Do not do a thing you may come to regret. This is not the way, Sarastro."

"It is the only way I can be sure," the voice said, a voice I now recognized as my father's. "And I've had almost sixteen years to think about it."

A figure stepped forward. In one hand, it carried the largest, brightest torch of all. So bright it made my eyes water and caused my mother to muffle her face inside her cloak. My first true sight of my father was thus obscured by tears, and I learned a lesson which I never forgot:

Darkness may cover light, but that is not the same as putting it out. Whereas, to overcome darkness, all light need do is to exist.

Yet, even beaten back, my mother was not cowed.

"This is not the way, Sarastro," she said again. "There is no need to do this, and the day may come when you will be sorry you have made this choice."

But my father simply laughed, the sound triumphant and harsh.

"Don't think you can threaten me with words, Pamina," he said. "It is simple. I have won, and you have lost. It was never much of a contest in the first place, really."

"It should never have been a contest at all."

"Enough!" my father cried. "I will not stand around in the dark and argue with you. Instead, I will simply take my daughter and go."

At this, I saw him give a signal, and I braced myself. I expected several soldiers to try and drag me from my mother's side. Instead a single man stepped forward. Even through the water in my eyes, I could tell he was the most handsome man that I had ever seen. Eyes the color of lapis lazuli. Hair that shimmered in the torchlight, almost as bright a gold as mine. He extended one hand toward me, as if inviting me to dance.

"Give me your hand and come with me," he said, "and I swear to you that your mother will not be harmed. Resist, and there is no telling what will happen."

And, in this way, I learned a second lesson I never forgot: Beauty may still hide a treacherous heart.

"What do you take me for?" I asked, and I did not hold back the scorn in my voice. "I will not give you my hand. For to do so is to give a pledge. This, I think both you and the Lord Sarastro know full well.

"I will not be tricked into pledging myself to a stranger. But I will come with you for my mother's sake, for I love her well and would not have her harmed."

"Strong words," my father said.

"And a strong mind to back them up," my mother replied. "I say again, you will regret this act, Sarastro. Thrice I have said it, and the third time pays for all."

"Step away from your mother, young Pamina," the Lord Sarastro said. "I will not ask again. Instead, I will compel."

And so, I stepped away, pulling my hood down over my face, for I had begun to weep in earnest and did not want to give my father and those who did his bidding the satisfaction of seeing me cry. The second I stepped away from my mother, I could feel the wind begin to rise. Tugging on my cloak with desperate, grasping fingers. Howling like a soul in hell.

Over the scream of the wind, I heard my father shouting orders in a furious voice. Then I was gripped by strong arms, lifted from my feet, and thrown like a sack of potatoes over someone's shoulder.

The last thing I saw was the flame of my father's torch, tossing like some wild thing caught in a trap.

The last thing I heard, dancing across the surface of the wind like the moon on water, was a high, sweet call of bells.

Bird Song

The Lady Mina has given me my cue, and so, just when you are wondering what happens next to her, I must doom you to disappointment, at least for a little while. For now it is time for me to enter and take up the story.

What cue, you are no doubt wondering?

She has called you intelligent. I know she has. Not only that, I know it pleased you. Don't bother to deny it. I know much more than I appear to, particularly if it has to do with Mina's story, for parts of it are also mine. Our tales are wrapped together, twisted around one another like point and counterpoint. Melody and harmony. But as for me, I'm not so sure how smart you are. How clever can you be if you failed to see my entrance coming?

She used the oldest trick in the book. The very last thing she said. How much easier did you want her to make it for you?

That's right. It's the bells that announce my entry into this story. I'm the one playing them, for they are mine. And who am I, you are no doubt wondering? I am Lapin, a name that means rabbit, though, fortunately, in a language not my own. There's a bit of irony for you. I couldn't care less about rabbits, unless they're in a stew.

It's the birds I care about.

See, this is where that great intelligence of yours is going to get you into trouble. You're trying to make sense of this, when it would really be so much better not to. Some things cannot be reasoned out, though they may be explained, a thing I will do shortly. In the meantime, you must do what I have learned to do: accept things as they come along without making too much of a fuss about them.

So just believe me when I say that I am called Lapin the bird catcher. Though, I prefer bird caller, if the truth were to be told. It's not precisely accurate to say that I *catch* birds. I don't set snares or traps. I don't lure them or capture them by force.

What I do is play my bells and the birds come to me. To wherever I am, from wherever they are. And once they have come, they never depart. This is how I came to know the Lady Mina.

But I'm getting ahead of myself.

I need to explain about the bells, and to do that, I must back up. The first member of my family to possess them was my grandmother. Though, as they never would have come to her had it not been for the actions of her own father, I suppose I must back up one step further to my great-grandfather. His name was Pierre-Auguste, and he was unlucky in love.

This is hardly an unusual circumstance. And,

when it does occur, the disappointed party is generally considered to have two options. He can pull in his breath and expel it in a laugh, thereby ensuring that his heart will mend and his life will go on. Or he can pull in a breath and expel it in a sigh, a signal that his heart will remain broken for as long as it continues to function. It was this second path that my great-grandfather chose.

But Pierre-Auguste did not stop there. He cherished his heartbreak, nourishing it like a sick child, until, with time, both it and he became something else altogether. A thing like the rind of a grapefruit left out in the sun. Hard and bitter. Sour enough to cut your mouth on.

In spite of this, he married, hoping for sons to carry on his name. He got a daughter, and at that, only one. A thing which, as the years passed, caused my great-grandfather's bitterness to increase to such an extent that it completely slipped its bounds. One day, he struck a servant, over nothing more important than the breaking of a teacup. She fell, and in so doing, pierced her temple upon the sharp edge of a table. She was dead before she hit the floor. And now, at long last, the powers who watch over the universe decided enough was enough. It was time for them to get involved.

Yes, there are powers who do this. Watch over the workings of the universe, I mean. I've never met any of them in person, so I don't know what their names are. I'm not even certain that they *have* names. Not like you and I do, anyhow. The only thing I know for sure is that they don't interfere in the lives of mortals very often.

To see the entire universe at a single glance requires excellent vision. And so it was that the powers that watch over the universe saw something no one else would have noticed when they looked upon my great-grandfather. And this is what it was: that the break in the heart of Pierre-Auguste might provide an opening to mend a rift between two others. This is the real reason they decided to get involved.

And so they appeared before my great-grandfather, who was understandably startled, not to mention frightened. They coshed him on the head, thereby giving him pretty much the punishment he expected. But instead of striking him dead, they sent him a dream. A dream of what might have happened if, at the very moment he'd sucked in a breath at the pain of his own heartbreak, he had released it in a laugh instead of in a sigh.

All the things my great-grandfather had never known were in that dream, the life he had denied himself. He awoke with tears upon his cheeks, the first he had shed since he was a boy. And so it was that my great-grandfather came to experience the one kind of bitterness he had never known: the bitterness of remorse. And thus was he justly punished.

But this was not all. For my great-grandfather

had done more than blight his own life. He had taken the life of another. And so the powers that watch over the universe now turned to his descendant, to my grandmother. And, through her, to those whose lives had not yet been dreamed of, let alone begun.

This means me, of course.

The powers that watch over the universe gave my grandmother, then a young woman, a set of bells. In number, twelve. Mounted on a board of mountain ash. To be struck with a hammer whose head was polished stone cut from the mountain at the heart of the world. And this is what they told her about them: If she could hear the melody of her own heart and sound it out upon the bells, she would call to her side her heart's true match. Its one true love.

Kind of sappy. Yes, I know. Also somewhat predictable. Great, nameless powers often make pronouncements of this sort, or so I'm told. Deceptively simple too. Hearing the melody of your own heart, then rendering it up, is not such an easy matter. You can trust me on this one. I know.

Not only that, but in the meantime, while you're practicing, there are many other creatures who may be listening, and the melody you play may be the one that calls to their heart, even though it doesn't match your own. A thing my grandmother discovered the day the grizzly bear showed up in the garden.

The first she knew about it was a great screech issuing from the house next door. My grandmother didn't pay much attention at first. The neighbors on that side were always making noise about something or other. It was the ominous silence that followed the screech that finally got her notice. That and the great, dark shadow that had suddenly come between her and the morning sun.

My grandmother looked up from the bench upon which she was sitting. There was a grizzly bear standing at the edge of her vegetable garden. As grizzly bears are primarily carnivorous, it seemed reasonably safe to assume it hadn't come to pick greens for a salad. In fact, being eaten right there and then was pretty much the only thing that came to my grandmother's mind.

In her astonishment and fear, my grandmother let drop the hammer with which she had been playing upon the bells. It struck the largest one on its way to the ground. At the sound it made, the bear made not a roar, but a soft, crooning sound. Its dark eyes gazed straight into my grandmother's, as if beseeching her for something.

Slowly, hardly daring to breathe, my grandmother bent and retrieved the hammer. Then, her hand shaking so much she feared the hammer would slip back out again, she began to play the bells once more.

As she did, the grizzly gave a great sigh of perfect contentment, turned around three times just like the family dog, curled up and went to sleep in the sun. Right on the bed of zucchini, which turned out to be a fine thing as my grandmother had, as always, planted too many of them anyhow.

And in this way did she come to understand that playing your heart's true melody upon even so beautiful an instrument was a thing much easier said than done.

She didn't give up trying, of course. Would you? I thought not. Soon the grizzly was joined by a brown bear, a sun bear, and a beaver suffering from an identity crisis of magnificent proportion. It was right about then that the neighbors began to murmur the word *witch*, and my grandmother and great-grandfather, who was now much nicer, began to contemplate leaving town.

Fortunately for them, the next living, breathing thing my grandmother's attempt to get her song right summoned was a carpenter. A young man as finely made as any house he hoped to build, who looked at my grandmother with dreams of castles in his eyes. She looked him up and down and thought it over. The melody she had played upon the bells that day was as close as she had ever come to getting her heart's true song right. All things considered, she decided it was close enough.

She and the carpenter were married. Together with my great-grandfather, they moved to a nearby hillside with a pond for the beaver and lots of land for the bears to roam. My grandmother raised grapes, my grandfather built a house, many, many arbors, and, eventually, my great-grandfather's coffin. My grandmother put the bells away until her children should be born.

And if, sometimes, in the dead of night, she heard her heart beating in ever so slightly a different rhythm than that of her sleeping husband, my grandmother simply pulled the pillow over her head. She had made her bed, or, actually, my grandfather had. But my grandmother was content to lie in it beside him.

Eventually, my grandmother bore a set of twins, a girl and a boy. The boy marched away to war at an early age, leaving his sister, the girl who would become my mother, behind. She was in no hurry to try the magic of the bells. Not until she was a young woman, until the music of her heart became too much for her body to contain, did she sit in one of her father's many arbors and attempted to sound it out.

She, too, ended up summoning animals, though not such alarming ones as her own mother. Her first attempt to play the bells summoned field mice from miles in every direction. They gathered around the bench on which she was sitting, noses twitching, and regarded her with round, dark eyes. There were so many of them, the family cat ran away that very afternoon.

Her second attempt brought squirrels with tails like bushy feather pens. The third, possums so homely they made her glad the animals themselves didn't see all that well. By this time, I'm sure you've gotten the general idea, and so had my mother, to her great dismay.

It seemed her specialty was to be rodents of all shapes, sizes, and kinds.

This fact upset her so deeply she married the first man who came along. He happened to be a baker, which was a good thing because, in her distress over what her playing called to her, my mother forgot to eat half the time.

My grandfather built them a house, not far from his own. The baker built a brick oven in the backyard and set about doing what he did best. Soon the townspeople were deciding to overlook their concerns that witchcraft might run in our family. Instead, they concentrated their attentions on my father's bread and my grandfather's wine. My mother put the bells away on the highest shelf that she could find, which happened to be in the bedroom closet. And there they stayed, all but forgotten, until the day I was born.

On that day, a momentous event occurred, and I don't mean just my own arrival. My mother was in one of those lulls which occur during labor, brief spells between one round of pain and the next. She lay still in her bed, panting just a little as the late afternoon sun was warm upon the bed, exhausted from working so hard.

She had just begun to feel the grip of the next contraction, when she forgot about the pain entirely. More rabbits than she had ever seen in one place together abruptly leaped in through the open window, and ran across the room and out the bedroom door.

Before my mother could so much as draw a breath to shout my father's name, they were followed by a group of foxes, and then a swarm of bees. That was the moment my mother realized the bed had begun to tremble and then to shake. Within instants, the whole bedroom had begun to sway from side to side.

My mother found her voice and shouted for my father in earnest. He arrived just as the closet door went crashing back and the set of bells hurtled to the floor. They struck the ground in such a way that all twelve bells sounded at the selfsame time. At which the trembling of the earth ceased, and my parents stared at one another in open-mouthed astonishment.

Oh, yes, and I was born.

When she had recovered sufficiently to tell my father of the events immediately preceding my birth, Papa, who was somewhat superstitious, decided that we had received a series of omens impossible to ignore.

And so I was given the name Lapin, after the rabbits who had been the first to understand that something momentous was about to occur, and the right to play the bells, not when I turned sixteen, but from the very day that I was born.

Lapin Comes to the Point, Finally

Yes, I know. You should hope so. For heaven's sake, just calm down. I do have a tendency to take the long way around, I admit it. But melodies and stories both can be like that. Besides, it's not as if I don't have my reasons for telling things the way I do. If you don't know where you've already been, how can you know which way to go?

I didn't start playing the bells right away. Not in any truly musical sense, anyhow. I did bang on them at a very young age, a circumstance which ended up with me and my playing being relegated to the great outdoors. Children were allowed a bit more freedom when I was young than they are nowadays. I didn't even have a nursemaid, but no one seemed to worry that I'd come to any harm.

I wasn't likely to be attacked or carried off, after all. I was making far too much noise.

I was five when I called my first bird down from the sky. It was a chickadee, a bird whose song is its own name. One moment I was sitting on one of the comfortable wooden benches my grandfather had made, trying to sound out an actual tune for the very first time. The next, there was a flurry of wings, and a small bird appeared by my side.

It had a sharp black beak, gray wings, and a white breast. It regarded me first with one expectant, inky eye and then the other, cocking its black-capped head from side to side.

I knew the legend of the bells by then, of course. My father had assured this by making them the subject of many a bedtime story. I played the melody again, at which point the chickadee threw back its head, opened its throat, and harmonized. And as it did, though I was only five, I understood that my future would be filled with the songs of birds. From that day to this, that moment is still the happiest of my life.

The week after that, I played a song that summoned a red-bellied woodpecker. After that came a bird with a white body and a dark hood pulled over its head, looking for all the world as if it was in disguise. This was a dark-eyed junco, or so my grandfather informed me. These were followed in succession by a green jay, and, close upon its tail feathers, a blue one. Small birds all, as befitted my overall size at the time.

Then came wrens, sparrows, and warblers of all shapes, colors, and varieties. An indigo bunting as blue as a cold autumn sky. An oriole as yellow as newly churned butter. A cardinal with feathers as red as the bright drops of my own blood that I saw the day I accidentally cut my finger on the sharpest of my father's bread knives.

Sometimes, I would play a song and nothing seemed to happen. Days would go by. Then, without warning, and generally when I was engaged in something altogether different, there would come the flutter of bird wings. The sound of the bells, or so it seemed, could travel as far as any bird could fly.

Before too long, my grandfather, getting on in years but still hale and hearty, set to work building bird feeders and bird houses. I began to play the bells at all hours of the day or night. For I had heard an old woman who'd come to buy bread say that not all birds like to sing in the bright light of day. There are some who prefer the soft shadows of the night.

And here, at last, my story is about to intersect with Mina's. For it was in calling down a night bird from the sky that I first came to the attention of the Queen of the Night.

I have already told you how the house my grandfather built for my grandmother came to be located on a hillside near the town where they'd both grown up, with my parents' house close beside it. But, as is often the case with hills, the one on which our houses resided did not stand alone. It was one of a series of many hills, all rolling together until, from their very center, a tall mountain shot straight up.

Among the many tales whispered about this mountain was that it was the first in all the world.

The one, in fact, from which the world itself had sprung. And this was the reason, it was further whispered, that the mountain was the chosen dwelling place of Sarastro, Mage of the Day, and his consort, Pamina, the Queen of the Night.

Not that anyone had ever seen them, of course.

But it was spoken that, in the time when the world began, they had wed and chosen this mountain in which to dwell. Like all the local children, I was curious about these tales. But I never thought I'd discover the truth of them for myself.

I did so when I was eight years old.

On the night of my eighth birthday, in fact. In honor of the occasion, I had been allowed to stay up a little later than usual. As always, I had with me the set of bells. My parents had thrown me a wonderful celebration. My heart was full of joy. And so, after all the guests save my grandparents had departed, I did the thing I always did when my heart was full. I sat in the orchard with my family around me and attempted to play the music of my heart upon the bells.

I'm not sure I can describe the melody I played. It was born in my heart and, if it lingers, it is there alone, and not in my mind. But I do recall that, for a long time after I ceased playing, nothing happened, save that the sounds of the world around me grew silent and still, as if they, too, had listened to my song.

The silence stretched for so long that I had pretty much decided there was no bird song to answer it, or, if there was, it lived in a breast that was very far away from mine. I had just risen to my feet, the bells tucked beneath one arm, when I heard the sudden rush and sweep of wings. And then a voice so sweet and clear answered my music that I swear I felt my own heart skip a beat.

"Mercy upon us," I heard my mother whisper. "You've called down a nightingale. They do say that's the favorite bird of the Queen of the Night."

No sooner had my mother finished speaking than the nightingale swooped from the branch on which it had landed and alighted on my shoulder. From there, it refused to budge. Together with my family, I returned to the house and went to bed, the nightingale perched upon my headboard with its head tucked against its breast. It became a fixture in our household from that night on.

I never saw it during the day. But, for the next week, each day at precisely the moment the sun slipped over the horizon, the nightingale would appear with that same rush and sweep of wings, finding me no matter where I was. Though I cherished all the birds my playing summoned, I freely admit I harbored a special spot in my heart for this one.

One week to the day after my birthday, there came a night when the moon was no bigger than a crescent of cut fingernail floating in the sky. All day long, my mother was edgy, murmuring under her breath that it was on nights such as this that the powers of the Queen of the Night, whom she sometimes called *die Königin der Nacht,* were strongest.

More than that, on such dark nights it had long been whispered that die Königin der Nacht walked abroad. Many had felt her passing, though few had seen her. For only those to whom she wished to reveal herself had the power to see her in the dark.

And, sure enough, as soon as the sun slipped over the horizon in a riot of color, the Queen of the Night arrived.

Her coming made the hillside around my parents' house tremble as it had the day I was born, a thing that convinced my father that the events attending my birth had now come full circle. He only hoped we would all survive them.

How shall I describe her to you, die Königin der Nacht?

Even though I was only eight, my eyes were old enough to recognize her beauty, my heart steady enough to feel the beat of hers and know that it was filled with anger and sorrow in almost equal parts. Her dark hair streamed out from her head, so long and fine it seemed to mingle with the darkened sky. Beaten silver was the color of her eyes. They were filled with tears, and when she wept the tears slipped down her cheeks like a shower of stars.

In her arms, she held an infant. It, too, was crying.

"Selfish, foolish boy!" scolded the Queen of the Night. "Where is the bird that you have stolen from me? Speak quickly, or I will put an end to your miserable life!"

It was at this moment that the first of several very astonishing things happened, as if what was happening already wasn't astonishing enough. My mother, the same mother who'd panicked at the sight of a group of field mice, stepped in front of me, standing toe-to-toe with die Königin der Nacht.

"How dare you!" she shouted. "Stop threatening my son right this instant! He didn't mean to take anything from you. He's a good boy. Besides . . ."

Here, my mother reached behind her back, hands flapping as if searching for something. Understanding immediately, my father rushed forward, snatched the set of bells from my hands, and thrust them into my mother's. Triumphantly my mother whipped them around, holding them out before the Queen of the Night.

"It was *these* that summoned your bird down from the sky. They have been in this family for three generations, given to us by the powers that watch over the universe. I'm thinking that means we're under their protection. You'd better watch out."

What the Queen of the Night might have replied to this very remarkable speech none of us, not even she, were ever to know. For, at that moment, as it did each evening, the nightingale shot down from the sky. It settled into its usual position on my left shoulder.

"You picked a fine night to be a little late," I whispered as softly as I could, and felt the soft prick of its beak against my cheek. The wailing of the infant picked up a notch.

"You see? You see?" cried die Königin der Nacht. She held up the child. At this, the next very astonishing thing happened.

"Oh, for goodness' sake," my mother snapped in her most exasperated voice. She turned to me, thrusting the bells back into my arms. "Hold these," she commanded. "They're yours, after all."

Then she turned, took two steps forward, and snatched the crying infant from the Queen of the Night's arms.

For the span of eight heartbeats, the same number of years that I had lived, nobody else did anything at all.

"There now, there now," my mother crooned to the infant as she rocked it gently, a thing that only seemed to make it wail all the louder. I saw die Königin der Nacht pull in a breath.

We are all about to die, I thought.

That was the moment the nightingale fluttered from my shoulder to my mother's, threw back its head, and began to sing a song so beautiful I swear it made the stars come out. The infant abruptly stopped wailing, hiccuped exactly once, and began to suck its thumb.

"There now," my mother said again as she gazed

down at the infant in perfect satisfaction. As for me, I kept my eye on the Queen of the Night. I wasn't so certain she was finished with us yet.

"This is my daughter, Pamina," die Königin der Nacht said after a moment, in a voice just like anyone else's. "The nightingale was singing, just as it is now, at the moment she was born. Ever since, it has had the power to soothe her, a power even stronger than a mother's love. But, a week ago, the bird flew from my side and did not return. Since then, my daughter and I have had no rest, by day or by night."

"She's beautiful," my mother answered. "But I think that she's too warm." She pushed the cloak in which the baby Pamina was swaddled back from her head. "Oh my."

Beneath the cloak, the baby's hair wasn't dark like her mother's, a thing I think we had all expected, but bright and shining as the morning sun, curling up from her head like steam rising from water set to boil. And in this way, I saw the beauty of the Lady Pamina for the very first time.

"So it is true what the old tales say," my father murmured, speaking up at last. "Night and day are joined together, and they have made a child."

"As you see," the Queen of the Night replied. "But until she turns sixteen, she is mine alone, to raise as I see fit. To prepare her for what is to come. But I'm hardly going to get anywhere if I can't even get her to go to sleep at the proper time."

She turned her beaten-silver eyes on me.

"Please," she said, and I heard my mother catch her breath. "Release the nightingale. Let her come home."

I tried to open my mouth, to explain the way I thought things worked, and discovered I couldn't move my jaw. The Queen of the Night, die Königin der Nacht, had just said please. How on earth could I say no?

It was the nightingale who finally helped me out. With a great cascading waterfall of notes, she ended her evening song. The Lady Pamina was, by this time, fast asleep in my mother's arms. The nightingale now left my mother's shoulder and returned to mine. She bumped her round, soft head against my jaw, as if to knock some sense into it.

"If you please, Your Majesty," I managed to get out.

"Pamina," said die Königin der Nacht. I think she was trying to put me at ease by letting me know her name was the same as her daughter's. I wasn't so sure it helped any, though. The most powerful being I had ever encountered, was ever likely to encounter, had just given me permission to call her by her first name.

It was all a bit much for an eight-year-old.

"If you please, Your Majesty Pamina," I said, and was rewarded by the glimmer of a smile. "I would if I could, but I don't think I can."

Not particularly eloquent, I admit, but it did get

the point across. Not only that, I'd managed to mean *no* without actually having to say it right out loud.

The Queen of the Night's dark eyebrows drew together. "Explain," she said. "Why not?"

"No bird who has ever come to me has left me again, not for good," I said. "I don't know why. I'm sorry."

"It's the bells," my father said. "The sound of them just plain gets inside your heart. If their sound calls to you, then you must answer. More than that, it is your wish to answer, just as it becomes your wish to dwell forever with the player of the bells.

"The bird stays not because my son keeps her captive, but because there is no other place that she would rather go. Wherever he is, that is now the place where she belongs. She cannot return to you, not in the way you wish. The bells have called and she has answered. The nightingale has given, and been given, her heart."

"That is it exactly," my grandfather put in.

The Queen of the Night was silent for a very long time.

"I perceive that you speak the truth," she said at last. She opened her arms, and my mother placed the sleeping Pamina into them. "What, then, shall become of my daughter?"

"Ow! All right!" I cried.

Five pairs of eyes turned in my direction, four mortal and one a great deal more. But they all did exactly the same thing: They stared straight at me and at the nightingale perched upon my shoulder. I'm sure she was doing her best to look innocent, assuming that's a thing a bird can actually accomplish. She'd just given me a sharp jab with her beak. It was this that had prompted me to cry out.

"I have an idea," I went on now. "I'm older than the Lady Pamina, so I must go to bed much later than she does. What if I come every night, just at bedtime? The nightingale will follow me and sing the baby to sleep. Then all will be well."

"Ah!" exclaimed die Königin der Nacht, and her gaze shifted away from me to my mother and father. "I begin to see why your son has called to him the most beautiful song on earth. He has a generous heart. What is your name, boy?"

"I am called Lapin, Madam," I answered.

The Queen of the Night's dark eyebrows flew straight up. "Your name means rabbit, yet you call down birds from the sky?"

"It's a long story," I replied. "But, if you please, I really do prefer Lapin. Not everybody knows that it means rabbit. Not everyone around here, anyhow."

The Queen of the Night nodded, and I could have sworn I saw a twinkle in her eye.

"Very well. I understand. I thank you for your generous offer, Lapin, but I'm afraid it is impossible. You can't travel back and forth from your home to mine. The distance is simply too great, even on a swift horse. If your parents and grandparents were willing to consider such a thing, however, there might be another option. You all could come and live with me."

"No," my mother said at once. "Not that we aren't grateful for the honor you bestow upon us, Lady, but we belong here." She reached for my father's hand, and he moved to clasp hers. "This is the life that we have chosen."

"You have chosen it, and chosen well," replied die Königin der Nacht. "But surely your son has a life of his own. Will you deny him? In my house he will have greater scope to discover what his heart holds. And what, in time, it may call to him."

"No," my mother said again. "He is just a boy."

"Please, *Mutter*," I said, surprising everyone present, myself most of all. "Let me at least try. I want to go."

And, as I said this, I realized how much it was so.

"Oh, Lapin," my mother said.

"Do not grieve," said the Queen of the Night. "For I will send him back to visit you when the days are shortest, and his coming will brighten your lives when the dark is long. And this I promise, now and forever: Neither I nor any who belong to me will ever hold your son against his will. Are you content?"

"No," my mother answered honestly. "But it is fair, and I will learn to live with it."

And that is how I came to be a servant of die

Königin der Nacht and went to live in her great house which lies inside a mountain.

Though I missed my parents, I never regretted my choice. Die Königin let me do as I pleased, as long as the nightingale and I were there to sing the Lady Mina to sleep each night. I played the bells in every corner of her great house until the mountain itself rang with birdsong. I watched the Lady Mina grow to be a beautiful young woman. And, from a distance, I did what I could to keep my eye on my mistress's husband, the Lord Sarastro.

What he made of me, I never knew, for we never actually spoke. But it was impossible to live in my mistress's house and not be aware of his presence. Most people think it is the dark that lurks, sly and treacherous. But I tell you that I think it is the light. For it is always hovering, just over the edge of the horizon, waiting to leap out and strike you blind.

And so, the years passed, moving inexorably toward the moment when the Lady Mina would turn sixteen and leave behind the only life that she had known.

"What is it like, Lapin?" she said to me one night in the year in which she was fifteen years old. We were doing a thing we often did, gazing out the window of her mother's observatory. A full moon gazed back down. As always in the evening, the nightingale was with us, though the bird now preferred the Lady Mina's shoulder to my own.

"Is it hard to leave behind all that you have known?"

"What's hard is never having an evening free from questions," I said. For the Lady Mina always had at least one up her sleeve. At my reply, she smiled. "I left what I knew of my own free will," I said, "though I was just a boy at the time."

"And I may not. Because my departure is a bargain already made, one in which I had no part. That's what you mean, is it not?" the Lady Mina both pronounced and asked at once.

I hope her father loves her, I found myself wishing fervently. *But more than that, I hope he appreciates her, especially her quicksilver mind.*

"That is what I mean," I acknowledged.

She fiddled with the hem of one long sleeve, worrying it between her fingers.

"He'll probably marry me off to some sunburned oaf."

"Definitely a possibility," I said. "Allow me to suggest you take along a hat when you go."

She chuckled, and left the sleeve alone. "It's a great pity I can't stay here and marry you instead."

At this, I took up my stone hammer and played a soft tune upon the bells. Nothing in particular, just whatever came to mind. To mind, but not to heart.

"Do you think that we belong together, then?" I asked. "That my heart calls to yours?"

The Lady Mina sighed. "No, Lapin. I think as I believe you do. That our hearts do not call to one another, though we love each other well. But it doesn't stop me from wishing that I need not marry a stranger."

"Then don't," I said, and I struck a brave sound upon the bells. "Don't be docile about all this. Be stubborn. Insist that you be allowed to marry the choice of your heart and no other."

"Easy for you to say," the Lady Mina said.

I ran the hammer along the bells, from high note to low, from top to bottom. The sound it made was jumbled and not at all harmonious.

"You think so?" I asked. For, though I was eight years older than Mina was, no song I had ever been able to play had brought me anything other than another set of wings.

"Of course not," the Lady Mina said at once. "I'm sorry. I'm out of sorts and taking it out on you. Pay no attention to me."

"I won't," I said. "I almost never do, you know."

This won a chuckle from her, as I had hoped. "Oh, Lapin," she said impulsively. "What would I do without you?"

"That is a thing you will never need to know."

She turned her head and looked with both her eyes into both of mine. I'm one of the few people who will meet her eyes, for a reason I will let her tell you herself at the proper time.

"Is that a promise?" she asked softly.

"It is a promise," I replied.

"I will hold you to it. You know that, don't you?"

"Of course I know that," I said. "Why else do you think I said it? Unless you doubt me."

"No, Lapin," the Lady Mina said. "I would never doubt you. Now let's both stop talking, shall we? Let me hear some music instead."

And so I sat and played the bells until the moon went down.

A week later, the Lord Sarastro took her away. A thief in the night, he stole her from her mother before the proper time. I saw it all, but could do nothing to prevent it. Even with my aid, die Königin, her daughter, and I would have been but three against many. Easily overcome.

Never will I forget the look upon my mistress's face as the louts with their blazing torches departed, bearing away the daughter whom she loved. Always its image will stay with me, even if I live until the end of time.

"Do you see, Lapin?" she cried when the lights had gone, when she could shake back her cloak and I could leave my hiding place, for all was dark once more. Tears as hard and clear as diamonds streamed down her pale cheeks. She was weeping a fortune, and why shouldn't she? Had she not just been deprived of the first treasure of her heart?

"Do you see what he has done?"

"I see," I said. "Now what shall *we* do?"

At this, she laughed, and the sound was wild, matching the sound of the wind as it rose. The second the Lady Mina had stepped away from her mother it had started, answering the call of the storm in my mistress's heart.

"Lapin," die Königin der Nacht said. "The name which means rabbit."

"It does," I said. "But that does not mean I have the brains of one. I've understood for many years now the real reason you brought me here. It was because you feared this day would come."

"Then you know what I would have you do," she said.

"I do," I answered. "But I warn you, I don't think this has ever been done. I cannot truly control what I may call. Furthermore, once I have begun, you cannot intervene on your daughter's behalf. It must be that which I summon, or nothing."

"I know these things," die Königin der Nacht said impatiently. "Why do you waste time telling me what I already know?"

"I just want us to be sure," I said. "There's always the chance that what I call will end up being even worse than what her father has in mind."

"Impossible," die Königin der Nacht proclaimed. "For I think you see my daughter truly, and I know you love her well. Both those things, I fear, are more than I can say for the Lord Sarastro. Bring my daughter the one who will set her free, as you brought the one who lulled her to sleep so long ago.

"Do it, Lapin. Play the bells."

⸎ What Lapin's Bells Summoned ⸎

What would have happened if there'd never been a storm?

If there'd never been a storm, I might never have heard the bells. And if I'd never heard the bells, I would never have entered Mina's life, an event that changed the lives of all.

I wonder about these things sometimes.

Foolishness, of course. If something is meant to happen, then it will. That's just the way the world works. There's no use trying to stop it or get around it. You probably know this for yourself. Fortunately, not everything that happens carries the same weight as everything else. Was I meant to hear the bells and enter Mina's story when I did? Absolutely.

Was I meant to eat the last piece of royal chocolate birthday cake before my younger brother, Arthur, could get to it, when I was ten and he was seven-and-a-half? Probably not. All that was required for that to happen was a willingness to get out of bed and creep down cold stone stairs in the middle of the night.

I can hear Mina's voice laughing in my ear.

Chiding me. *How can they follow your portion of this tale when you haven't even told them who you are?* And so I suppose I'd better get that out of the way. Things are no doubt confusing enough with so many different people telling you what happened.

I am a prince, and my name is Tern.

A tern is a seabird, something like a gull. Not even my parents have a good explanation for why this is the name I was given the day I was born. Neither of them had ever seen the sea before. The land my father governs lies many miles from any coast. Rivers we have in plenty. Also lakes, streams, swamps, and ponds. But you could ride for days on end on the swiftest horse in my father's stables and still not catch a glimpse of the sea. Yet a seabird is what I was named for.

If you decide to seriously press my mother, tell her you refuse to eat your broccoli until you get an explanation, she'll tell you that she named me Tern because she liked the sound. There's a problem with this. You can probably recognize it right off. All sorts of words may make lovely sounds when you speak them aloud: aubergine, tamarind, minaret, crevasse.

But the fact that they produce nice sounds doesn't mean they make good names. Who wants to be named after some great gaping hole in the ground? A name needs to fit, to have some meaning. At the very least it ought not to get in the way of the person on whom it's been bestowed. A name ought to help a person fulfill his destiny, help make it clear, not make it more complicated than it already is. Destiny is tricky enough, after all.

In the end this is precisely what my strange name did. It made my destiny clear. It simply took its own sweet time about it.

As I think I said earlier, my part in this story begins with the storm. A storm like no other any person in our kingdom had ever seen. A storm that made it seem as if the very night itself was in a rage, a fury of lust for revenge which would be spent only with the rising of the sun.

Stars shot across the heavens like stones from a thousand catapults. The wind screamed in fury and howled with pain all at the same time. Its strength caused slate to fly from the roofs of houses in the village which had stood, untouched, for centuries. Trees let go of their hold on the earth and flew into the air and out of sight.

The land trembled, and a great roaring came from everywhere at once, so that it seemed as if my homeland itself had been yanked from the earth as easily as the trees, and was even now being carried miles away to be deposited beside the sea.

Just when it seemed as if there could be no other outcome than that the world would tear itself apart, a single bolt of lightning, sharp and jagged as a javelin, shot straight down from the sky. It landed in the very center of the forest near my father's castle. The King's Wood, our people called it.

Then, with a final shriek of anguish, the wind went still. There was a moment of absolute silence. For no reason I could name, my heart began to beat in hard, quick strokes, as if I were more frightened now than I had been at the height of the storm. *Something has happened,* I thought. *Something important.* But I did not know yet what it was.

Then, from the castle courtyard below, I heard my father's voice calling for the lighting of torches. Quickly, for I knew I would be needed, I threw on a cloak and went down. The people of the village were just beginning to creep from their homes. Like one cat under the hostile eyes of another, they moved carefully and cautiously, as if they expected to be pounced upon.

"Ah, Tern," my father said when he saw me. "Good, there you are. Stay by me a moment, will you?"

He paused to watch my mother and her ladies-in-waiting set off to see if there were any wounded or ill who needed tending. My younger brother, Arthur, who is very good at such things, went to see if there was any rescuing to be done. Finally my father turned back to me.

"Tern," he said, his dark eyes sober in the torchlight. "Take these two"—he gestured to his two most faithful retainers—"and find out what has happened in the wood. Send them back to me when you know."

"Father, I will," I promised.

For, suddenly, I knew what the important thing that had happened was, or at least what my father feared it might be. I knew exactly what my father wanted me to look for. Exactly where to go. And so it was that half an hour later, my father's most faithful retainers and I discovered where the lightning had struck. We saw what it had done, and undone.

In the center of the King's Wood there stands—there stood—a great oak tree, the only one of its kind. It was so old no one could remember when it had been any smaller, let alone when it had been young. It was called the King's Oak. According to the legends of my land, it had been planted on the day our very first queen had borne her lord his very first son.

Over the years, the tales about the tree had grown even as the tree had, until it was almost as important a symbol to our people as the king himself. A change in the oak would mean a change in the kingdom, or so the people said, and they believed it. If it should be struck down, so should we all.

The bolt of lightning had split the King's Oak in two, straight down the middle, one side falling to the left, and one side to the right. In the light of our torches, my father's men and I could see that, on both halves, the heart of the tree had been exposed. It was still strong and hearty. Save for the lightning, the

King's Oak could have stood another number of untold years.

This was the good news, I suppose. But the bad news was that my father's fear had turned out to be well-founded. The lightning had struck the King's Oak. Clearly some great change was in store for our land. The only question was, what kind?

I pulled in a breath, turned my back on the tree and my face to my father's retainers.

"Return to my father the king and tell him this," I instructed. "The King's Oak lies in two pieces, yet even parted, it is strong. Say that I would have him return with you to see this for himself, so that he may decide what it means, and further, what should be done."

The retainers bowed and left me without a word, though I knew what they were thinking. They were afraid. Even by the light of their flickering torches, I could see it in their eyes.

It didn't take long for my father to return. Most of the village came with him, or so it seemed at the time. Soon the clearing around the King's Oak was as bright as day, filled with the light of many torches. Their flames were the only thing in the clearing that moved, save for my father himself and the eyes of his subjects as they watched him walk around the cloven tree once, twice, three times.

It was so quiet you could have heard a single leaf drop to the ground, had there been any left to fall.

There were not. All had been swept down by the storm.

Finally my father halted and turned to face his subjects. At this, the eyes of the people halted, too, and so did their breath. I think even their hearts stopped beating as they waited for my father to speak, to say what he thought the future held in store.

"My son, Prince Tern, has spoken truly," said my father. "The King's Oak lies split in two, yet, in both halves, the heart is strong. So does the strength of our kingdom hold true, for do I not have two sons, and are not their hearts strong?"

At this, a great sigh went through the clearing as all the people expelled their breath at once. My father had not pronounced the cleaving of the oak to be a disaster. This was the good news. Yet even a small child could see that we still had a problem.

"I believe we have been given a sign this night," my father continued, "and that it concerns my two sons. Both are strong and fit to rule when I am dead, yet the crown can pass to only one. Tradition would dictate that it must pass to my firstborn. But all of you know well what is spoken of the King's Oak: that, if it changes, our kingdom shall change, also.

"Therefore, hear what I have decided shall be done. Let Prince Tern choose one half of the tree. Let Prince Arthur choose the other. Then, let them fashion from the heart of the King's Oak what their own hearts summon. In the morning, I shall judge what each has made, and in this way will your future king be chosen."

"You choose first, Tern," Arthur said, before I could so much as open my mouth to suggest that he do likewise.

Now, the King's Oak had been split straight down the middle. You might not think it would make much difference which side of it I chose. But, as my father stood to make his decree, with his back to the tree and his face to his people, one half of the downed tree lay to his left side, and the other to his right.

Yes, of course, you are no doubt thinking, and no doubt with impatience. *How else would they fall?*

The point I'm trying to make is this: If I chose the left half, I chose the half closest to my father's heart. And in so choosing, I would make a statement, stake a claim: that I was the son whose heart was the most like my father's, and therefore most fit to rule when my father's heart beat no more.

This sort of thing is considered important where I come from. For my father believes, and I must admit that I agree, that the heart of a king is his most important attribute, not his proud bearing, his big voice, or even his fine mind. Any idiot in a decent suit of clothes may sit upon a throne, a thing usurpers have proved from time to time.

The best kings are the *true* kings. The ones born to rule. The ones who have known this was their destiny before they understood what it was they knew, for it commenced with the very first beat of their heart. And that's why regicide is such a terrible crime. A true king is a king in his heart, a heart which must be allowed to beat to the very end. To live its full and proper life. Only when the heart of a true king ceases to beat can the heart of his successor take its place.

As a general rule, that heart is expected to beat in the breast of his firstborn son. But every now and again, even nature can skip a beat, and the heart of a king will beat in a younger son. I had often wondered whether this was the case with Arthur and me, because of our names, if nothing else. I get named for the sea-gulls, most of whom are scavengers. My brother, for one of the most legendary kings of all time.

And so, after a hesitation that seemed like an hour but was, in fact, no longer than the time it took to take a breath, I bowed to my father and stepped to the tree's right side.

"I will choose the right," I said, "for the right hand of a king must be strong."

I heard a murmur of appreciation rise up from the people, and two other sounds. So soft I think only the three of us most closely concerned heard them. I heard my brother, Arthur, suck in his breath, and my father expel his in a sigh.

"And I will take the left," Arthur said, stepping forward in his turn. "The better to protect the king's heart."

"So be it," my father said. "I will judge what you have made at dawn."

Tern Makes a Choice and Hears a Sound

Swiftly my brother and I set to work. He on the left side of the King's Oak, and I on the right. My father and his subjects returned to the village, leaving Arthur and me alone within a ring of torches. What beat in my brother's heart during the rest of that strange night, I cannot tell. But in my own there pounded a desire more fierce than any I had ever known.

And it was simply this: to learn what my own heart might hold.

I could hear our father returning before I was finished. It was only then that I realized Arthur had been silent for some time. I turned, for we had been working back to back, and saw him sitting upon the ground. His head was bowed, as if in weariness. Across his lap lay a great spear, as long as the King's Oak was tall. And all carved from the heart of the left side of the tree.

Oh, well done, Arthur, I thought.

"You always have to try to be first, don't you?" I said. "It wasn't a race, you know."

At this, Arthur looked up with a smile, for this was an old joke between us.

"Still trying to compensate for the order of my birth," he replied. Then his face grew serious. "Tern," he began. "About the half of the tree you chose—"

"Arthur," I interrupted him. "Please, don't say anymore. I chose the right half." At the unintended pun, I made a face. "The *correct* half," I went on. "You know it, and I know it. I think even Papa knows it. Why else would he have come up with this particular test for us?"

"He could just want to see what kind of woodcarvers we are," Arthur remarked, his tone mild.

"Good gracious!" I exclaimed in perfect imitation of our mother. "I hadn't considered that."

"Old idiot," Arthur said.

"Young moron."

I cuffed him on the ear. He poked me in the stomach with one end of that impossibly long spear. We were standing with our arms around each other's shoulders, grinning like buffoons, when our parents arrived.

"Oh ho," my father said when he saw us. "So now you've decided the fate of our kingdom is just one big joke?"

"He started it," Arthur said.

"Did not."

"Did too."

"My sons," my father said sternly, though his face twitched strangely, a surefire sign that he was fighting back a smile. "Enough. The people will be here soon and we must not confuse them with mischievous behavior. They're already worried enough."

"Yes, Father," Arthur and I said in unison, a thing which made my father's face twitch once more.

Arthur and I stepped apart. I could see my mother, who had, naturally, accompanied my father, looking first at Arthur and then at me. When she looked at my brother, her eyes were dry. When she looked at me, she had tears in her eyes. And so it seemed that the only people who did not know that the matter of who would succeed my father was already settled were his subjects.

They crowded into the clearing now, their faces wary, yet expectant. Together, my parents stepped back to stand among them, facing me and Arthur.

"My sons, have you completed the task I set?" my father asked, his tone formal.

"Father, we have," I responded.

"As Prince Tern chose his portion of the tree first, let Prince Arthur be the first to show what he has made."

"As the king commands," my brother said, and he stepped forward.

"I have made a spear," he said as he knelt and offered it to my father. "As long as the King's Oak is tall."

"And why have you done this?" my father asked as he took it from him. He hefted it, as if testing the weight, judging how far it would fly when thrown.

"So that there should be no portion of our land that my arm cannot protect in time of peace or defend in time of war," my brother responded.

"This is well done," my father said. And he gestured for Arthur to rise. He handed him back the spear. Arthur accepted it, then returned to my side.

"What have you made, Prince Tern?" my father asked.

And it was only as he asked the question that I realized something. An important something. A something you would have thought I'd realized before now: I didn't know. My heart had been so full of the desire to know itself that I hadn't even noticed what my hands had carved.

I looked down at them now.

"A flute," I said. *A flute? Oh, for crying out loud.* This was a bit eccentric, even for me, particularly after Arthur's very manly spear.

"And why have you done this?" my father asked, just as he had asked my brother.

I did the only thing I could. I pulled in the deepest breath my lungs would hold, looked my father straight in the eye, and told the truth.

"My lord," I said, "I truly do not know. I listened to my heart when carving from the tree, and the flute is what my heart called forth."

I think even my father was somewhat at a loss for words at this. It's difficult for someone who has always recognized their destiny to hear the words, "I do not know." Fortunately for all concerned, my mother chose this particular moment to speak up.

"Let us hear you sound it," she said. "Perhaps, then, we all shall know."

"As the queen commands," I replied.

"Say as she *requests*, rather," my mother said, and she smiled.

And so I pulled in a second breath, as deep as the one I had just taken, lifted the flute to my lips, and began to play.

It's hard to describe what happened next. I think the simplest thing to say is that, for me at least, the world around me was no longer the world I knew. Or rather, it was the world I knew, but so much more.

My mind knew that I was standing in the King's Wood, facing my parents and my father's assembled subjects, with my brother at my side. My mind knew that there was grass beneath my feet and trees in a great circle all around. It even knew that I felt both foolish and afraid, for I was far from understanding what was going on.

But my heart . . . My heart registered none of these things, for it was filled with sound.

I cannot tell you what melody I played. I'm not so sure it was one you would recognize. Instead, it was as if the voice of the flute was the voice of the wide world itself and the beating of my own heart, all at once. Playing was like running as hard and fast as I could, simply for the joy of it. Like standing absolutely still with my bare feet in the waters of a clear, calm lake, with my face tipped up to face the sun.

Like starlight. Like moonlight. Like nothing I had ever experienced or could ever hope to describe. As if all the possibilities I could ever dream of, as well as countless others which had never even occurred to me, had suddenly become crystal clear and transformed into sound.

That was the music the flute made. And at the moment I ceased to play, I understood the truth: I had been playing the music of my heart. And no sooner did I understand this than I heard a new sound seizing the fading notes of the flute, as if it had been chasing after them. Holding on to linger when the sound of the flute was done.

Faint, yet clear, I heard the chime of bells.

Slowly I brought the flute down from my lips. The look upon my father's face was one that I had never seen before.

"I believe that Death himself would stop to listen to such music," my father said.

And, suddenly, for the first time ever, I saw into my father's heart, and saw that it was filled with doubt. Strong and true as Arthur was, it might be no bad thing for me to succeed my father after all. For the flute that I had made might inspire the people I ruled to greatness. Might halt an enemy without the spilling of a single drop of blood.

That was when I heard it again, louder this time: the high, sweet call of bells. The sound they made seemed to set my whole heart jangling, so near, so very near it was to my heart's own song. And at that moment, I knew what I must do. If I was ever to search out my own destiny, find the one whose heart beat with mine, I had to set out. Right now.

"My lord," I said, and I went to kneel before my father as my brother had done. "I honor you, and I honor this land. But as you commanded me to carve what I would from the heart of the King's Oak, now let me say what is in my own heart."

"I pray you, do so," my father said. And he stooped and put his hands on my shoulders, urging me to rise.

"Father," I said when I had gotten to my feet. "Let my brother, Arthur, be king when you are gone. For his heart bids him to stay, while mine urges me to go. I cannot be a good king, a true king, if my heart lies elsewhere, no matter how much I love our land or the people I would govern."

"Is this truly what your heart speaks?" my father asked.

"It is," I answered steadily. "I swear this on my honor, as your son."

"Then so be it," my father said. He embraced me, stepped forward to embrace my brother, then, with one arm around my shoulder and the other around

Arthur's, he turned all three of us to face the assembled crowd.

"Hear now, all of you!" he cried. "Prince Tern will travel through the wide world, listening to the music of his heart until he discovers what it may hold. Then, with all my heart, I hope he may return to us once more.

"Prince Arthur will succeed me. He will rule in this land after I am gone. Now let the kingdom be filled with rejoicing, for the riddle of the King's Oak is solved!"

"Long live Prince Arthur!" the people shouted. Caps flew into the air. Children clapped their hands as they were hoisted up onto shoulders. "Long live Prince Tern!"

"I'll thank you to notice they said my name first," Arthur murmured as my father went back to stand beside my mother, leaving the two of us to stand waving at the crowd.

"They're just brownnosing," I murmured back. "You're going to be king, after all."

At this, Arthur gave a shout of laughter, and the people hoisted us up onto their shoulders and carried the two of us home through the dawn.

Shortly after a good breakfast, in which it seemed to me the entire kingdom took part, I tucked the flute into a pocket of my tunic right above my heart and pulled a well-provisioned knapsack upon my back, for I am not entirely without good sense. Then I set out to answer the call of the bells.

The Lady Mina Speaks Her Mind

Fear.

I could feel it in the arms that held me. Taste it on the tip of my tongue. Hear it in the sound of the wind as it tore through the trees. Fear and pain and rage combined.

My fear. My pain at the duplicity of my father. The breaking of my mother's heart. The fear of my father's soldiers. Where the rage came from, I could not tell. But, every now and then, like a flash of sheet lightning against a pitch-black sky, came an emotion that stood alone, and this one was easy to identify: It was the Lord Sarastro's triumph.

Just when I was sure my ribs would break from being bounced against the hard shoulder bone of the one who held me, I heard a barked command, and the company halted. Almost at once there came a great clang, like the raising of a portcullis. There was a second command, and, again, we moved forward. As we did so, I heard the hard-soled boots of the soldiers ring out upon stone. Since I was facedown, I could easily see the way that sparks flew up, so smartly did they march inside the Lord Sarastro's dwelling place. With a second clang, the great doors of iron closed behind us.

Trapped, I thought.

"Set her down," said the Lord Sarastro. "But bring her along."

At once, I was set on my feet. One strong hand remained on my arm. It propelled me through a series of narrow corridors so swiftly, it was all I could do not to stumble. Then, with a suddenness that reminded me of the way the earth will sometimes abruptly fall away on both sides of a twisting mountain path, the walls of the corridors winged back and a great hall yawned before us.

I could tell this mostly by the feeling of immense open space, by the way the room *felt,* not because I could see it for myself. My hood was still pulled over my face, so low I could see nothing save when I gazed straight down.

"Release her," the Lord Sarastro said. And, at his command, the hand fell away. I heard the scrape of a boot as my captor stepped back. I was left standing alone.

Of course my first impulse was to push my hood back, the better to study my new surroundings. Or, if not that, then at least to stare with open defiance at the man who, within the last few moments, I had decided I would never call father.

I did nothing.

Instead, I kept my head bowed, my hands folded

inside the sleeves of my cloak. For it came to me without warning, as inspiration often does, that my silence might be a weapon I could use in whatever battle I was about to fight with the Lord Sarastro. That there must be a battle seemed obvious.

He had broken the agreement made at my birth, broken his own oath. Set his will against my mother's and broken hers into pieces. But he had yet to learn how strong my own will was.

"Welcome, my daughter, Pamina," the Lord Sarastro said. "Welcome to your new home."

And, at his words, I felt my legs begin to tremble as a terrible emotion seized my whole body.

You are wrong, my lord, I thought. *I cannot have a new home, for I never had an old one. A home is a place one's heart creates and so recognizes as its own. A place it enters of its own free will. All others are merely dwelling places.*

I bit my lip to keep from crying out my pain, for it seemed to me, in that moment, that I saw my future spreading out before me. My father would marry me to some stranger of his own selection, a man who matched the criteria of the Lord Sarastro's heart but not mine. I would spend my life in the dwellings of others. I would never know my own true home.

The pain of this realization stopped up my voice, so I made no answer to the Lord Sarastro's welcome.

"Let me take you to your room," he finally said

when it became clear that I would not reply. "Perhaps, when you have had a chance to rest, you will see that all will be well."

How can it be, when it has begun like this? I thought. Though the truth was that the pain of this moment had been started long ago, in the moment my parents first turned away from one another.

He must have made some signal, for, again, I felt that strong hand upon my arm. It piloted me across the great hall and toward a flight of stairs. As I lifted my foot to place it upon the first step, I suddenly cried out, for, as the torchlight fell upon the stair, light leaped into being, a light so bright it all but dazzled my eyes. Some vivid mineral flecked the stone, sleeping deep within until awakened by the light of the torch.

"This is porphyry," the Lord Sarastro said as he paused to let me catch up. "Do you know it? It is beautiful when the light shines upon it, don't you think?"

It is, I thought. *And it is not.* It seemed even the steps beneath my father's feet had been created to prove a point, the same point he had driven home to my mother by snatching me away. No matter how strong, no matter how beautiful, dark would always be overcome by light.

And so, for the third time, my father, the Lord Sarastro, spoke to me and I said nothing. But beside me, I heard the one who held me make a sound. In one ear and out the other before I could determine what it meant.

"Statos," my father said as if he'd understood precisely. "That will do. You must give her time."

Statos. The golden one, I thought. The one who had tried to trick me into giving him my hand. And I knew then what my father had in mind. There would be no parade of potential husbands. There would be no need. He already had the one he wanted.

Without another word, my father turned and continued to the top of the stairs, a servant lighting the way before, Statos and I following behind.

At the top of the stairs was a wide, curved corridor of white marble, gleaming like a river of milk in the light of the torches. Open to the air and bordered by a low balustrade on the left and by the stone wall of the mountain itself on the right. The Lord Sarastro moved down it at a brisk pace, so swiftly I almost had to run to keep up, an action which caused my hood to slip back. For the first time, I began to get a better look at my surroundings.

A row of illuminated sconces lined the wall on the right. Between them were hung tapestries depicting the course of the sun across the sky. Like the stairs which I had climbed to reach this place, the background of each tapestry was dark. But the sun was embroidered in gold thread so that it flashed in the light.

At the far end of the corridor, my father stopped.

In front of him was a single door. At his nod, the servant knocked once, then threw it open and stepped inside. My father waited until I had reached him.

"This will be your room, Pamina," he said. "If not tonight, then one day soon, I hope that you will find it to your liking."

Then, with a gesture that I should go first, he ushered me inside. It was like walking into a jar of honey, warm and golden. The floor was burnished amber. Great swathes of gleaming silk just a shade lighter adorned the walls. A bright fire burned in a black iron grate, with a great overstuffed chair and matching footstool pulled invitingly in front. An enormous bed covered in ivory damask stood on a raised dais in one corner.

But it was the windows that drew me most of all. One entire wall of lead-paned glass. *How it will sparkle in the sun!* I thought. Even now, the stars shone through, beautiful and hard as diamonds.

"How many times must I tell you to draw the curtains at night, Gayna?" I heard my father's voice say. And it was only then I realized that the room was already occupied.

She was tall, dark-haired, and beautiful. But then I knew these things already, for I had seen her often enough. At the sight of her, my heart gave a strange twist. This was the girl my father had raised instead of me, the forrester's child.

He has given me her room, I thought.

"I beg your pardon, my lord," she said, and she moved toward the windows.

"Why not leave things as they are?" a new voice proposed. Deep and smooth as the velvet drapes for which Gayna's long fingers were even now reaching. *Statos,* I thought. His voice was like the color of the room, warm and golden as honey.

"Your daughter is accustomed to the night, my lord. Perhaps seeing one thing which is familiar will make this transition easier for her."

He was right, of course. Not that I liked him for it. I saw the girl, Gayna, hesitate, as if uncertain which man she wished more to please.

So that is the way things are, I thought.

"Very well," the Lord Sarastro said, though I could tell by the sound of his voice he wasn't pleased. "But for this one night only. Pamina is my daughter, as much as she is her mother's. Not only that, she lives with me now. That is a fact to which she must grow accustomed. The sooner the better."

He talks about me as if I wasn't even here, I thought.

Gayna's hand dropped to her side. The room filled with silence.

"I will leave you now, daughter," the Lord Sarastro went on. "Gayna will stay with you this one night, so that you will not be lonely. In the morning, I will send for you."

I laughed before I could help it. I didn't mean to, but the sound rose up and out, quick and bitter, before I even knew that it was forming.

"You're worried that I'll be lonely?" I asked, and I made no attempt to hide the derision in my voice. The disbelief. "Don't you think it's a little late to be concerned about that?"

In the shocked silence that followed, I heard a piece of wood snap inside the grate.

"So you can talk," the Lord Sarastro said, his voice curiously mild. "I was beginning to wonder."

"You should not speak so to the Lord Sarastro," Gayna burst out, as if she couldn't hold back her outrage for one second longer. "You owe him your respect, your allegiance, and your love. He is the Mage of the Day. He is your father."

"He is an oath-breaker," I replied.

And then, as if her rebuke had broken a dam inside me, all the hot words I had been storing up came streaming forth.

"An oath-breaker," I said again. And now, at last, I pushed my hood all the way back, so that all could see my face clearly, though my hair was still bound up in its dark scarf. I heard Statos hiss out a breath through his perfect white teeth. Save for the fire, it was the room's only sound.

This is how my father, the Lord Sarastro, seemed to me now that I looked upon him without tears, and with my eyes wide open: He looked for all the world like a lion in his prime. A full beard covered the lower half of his face, exactly the same color as the chestnut hair which curled back from his forehead, then tumbled down to brush his shoulders. He wore a doublet of bronze velvet. Upon his brow was set a circlet of beaten gold the same color as his eyes.

I felt a pain so sharp I feared my very bones would splinter and pierce my flesh. This was my father. All my life I had wanted him to know and to love me. The father whom, for all my life, I had wished to know and to love. If he had waited just a few more hours, who is to say what might have been possible between us? But he had not, and so I knew there could be nothing.

"By his own act, the Lord Sarastro has forfeited my respect," I said now, "and my allegiance, for one cannot pledge to serve where one does not trust. As for love . . ." I turned to face Gayna where she still stood by the window. I saw her eyes go wide as she looked into mine.

"Let us hope you love him enough for both of us," I said. "For that must suffice him, as I find I do not love him at all. I will never be governed by his will. Never marry a man of his choosing. I will never call him father.

"And, for the record, my name is Mina."

"So it is true what the tales say," Gayna whispered. "The daughter of the Queen of the Night bears the evil eye."

"Gayna!" the Lord Sarastro said sharply. "Enough!"

But I simply laughed once more. "And which one would that be?" I inquired sweetly. "The gold or the silver? You'll want to be careful how you answer, for you may reveal more about yourself than you know."

For this is what they all had seen, a thing I have not told you until now: My eyes are two different colors. One as silver as the stars, the other as golden as the sun. A daily reminder that I was a child of two worlds. Worlds who could not live without one another, yet could not get along.

"In your grief, you speak things you should not," the Lord Sarastro said, and, though I turned back to face him, I could not read the expression on his face, in his voice, or in his eyes.

"For tonight, I will be understanding. But my patience will end with the rising of the sun. At dawn, you will be presented to my subjects as my daughter, whether you desire this or not, for not even you can deny who you are.

"The life that you have known is over, Mina. The sooner you accept this fact, the better for you things will be." He turned away then, motioning with one hand. "Come, Statos."

For a moment, I thought that Statos would protest. That he would speak to me directly, make some plea. But he did not. Instead, he made me a formal bow. Then he followed my father out of the chamber, leaving Gayna and me alone.

The Thoughts of the Forrester's Dark-Haired Child

I didn't want to like her. That much should be obvious. I didn't even want to feel sorry for her, for sympathy is nothing more than the top of a steep and slippery slope.

So what did I want, you are no doubt wondering? The truth is that my desire was twofold. Preferably, that the daughter of the Lord Sarastro had never existed in the first place. But, if she had to, what I wanted more than anything under the sun was really quite simple.

I wanted to hate her guts.

I even managed it, for most of the first hour after we had been left alone. My anger, my outrage over the way she had spoken to her father was enough to carry me straight through that. It was as my anger began to fade that I began to perceive that I had a problem.

After her father and Statos's departure, the daughter of the Queen of the Night—I had already decided I would not call her *Mina,* not even in the privacy of my own mind—the daughter of the Queen of the Night moved to sit by the window, to stare out at I couldn't quite imagine what.

For what is there to see in a night sky, after all? It's nothing more than a dark blanket, stitched some nights with the moon and always with the stars. But, unlike the sun, which can pretty much be counted upon to do the same thing day after day, the night sky is as changeable as the one who governs it. Die Königin der Nacht.

The moon alters its shape, day by day, month by month. The stars change positions, dancing to the passage of the seasons. Never mind that such things can be predicted, even plotted out. You cannot trust the night sky. It's really as simple as that, in my mind. And in my heart, I know this truth: What cannot be trusted is difficult to love.

And so I sat on the bed, and the daughter of the Queen of the Night sat in a chair by the window. I looked at her. She looked at the night. I'm not sure when I realized that she had changed position, ever so slightly. She must have done it the one time I moved to stir up the fire. For the room was cold with the drapes pulled back from all those windows. A chill had taken possession of the air even though it was high summer. *Just another of night's perversities,* I thought.

But when I resumed my seat again, I saw that the Queen of the Night's daughter was resting her head against the cold windowpane, as if it had become too much effort to hold her head up. It was her only concession to the strain of what had happened to her this night.

But she did not speak. Not one word since her outburst to her father. I might have not existed at all for all the attention she paid me.

Perhaps that is her *wish,* I thought.

And with that thought, I made my very first mistake. For if she could make a wish, even if it was the opposite of anything I wished for, then she was not so very different from me, after all. I may be selfish. I admit it. But I am not stupid. And I've never been deliberately unfair, or at least I hadn't been at that point.

"What is that you see?" I asked, at long last breaking the silence. And this was my second mistake, a thing I probably don't need to tell you.

For, with this question, I had acknowledged many things. That I was curious. That I had let my curiosity get the better of me. But, most important of all, I think, I had acknowledged the fact that she might look upon the night sky and see things that I could not.

"Come and look for yourself," she said. She didn't even bother to lift her head from the windowpane. I stayed right where I was. But after a moment, she sat up straight and looked around. The light from the fire fell upon one half of her face, lighting up her golden eye like a new-struck coin. The eye of silver, the one that belonged to the night, was closest to the window, indistinguishable from the light of the stars.

"Unless you are afraid, of course."

There's a reason that this is pretty much the oldest trick in the book, and that would be because it works almost every time. I could almost feel the spurt of anger that pushed me to my feet and across the room toward her, even as my mind urged me to stay right where I was.

"I'm certainly not afraid of you," I said.

She turned back to the window as I approached, but not before I thought I saw the flicker of a smile. Not a smile that triumphed over me, just a lightening of her expression. I suppose it could have been a trick of the firelight, but I really don't think so.

"Then look," she said, "and I'll tell you what I see with my eyes, if you tell me what you see with yours."

"Fair enough," I said. I nudged her feet from the footstool upon which they had been resting and sat down upon it so that, for all intents and purposes, we were sitting side by side.

"Oh, my," I said after a moment.

"Exactly what I was thinking," said the daughter of the Queen of the Night.

"It doesn't do this often, does it?"

I heard, rather than saw her shake her head, for, now that I had dared to look, I couldn't tear my eyes away from the night sky. Never, not even on the clearest night I could remember, had I seen so many stars. Nor had I ever seen any behave in quite this way.

They were falling from the sky. Each and every one.

Some shot from one side of the window clear

across to the other, as if chasing one another, racing around in circles, desperate to tire themselves out. Others arced up, like divers leaping off high cliffs, then shot straight down.

Earlier, during the time in which I now knew the Lord Sarastro had first laid hands upon his daughter, there had been a terrible storm. Trees had writhed as if in agony. The wind had made so terrible a sound I'd wanted to crawl straight underneath my bed and stay there until morning.

Frightening as that was, this was even worse, for it all happened without a sound. Below, the world was absolutely still, while in the heavens above, the stars committed suicide.

It was the most beautiful, the most bitter thing that I had ever seen. For it seemed to me I understood its cause.

The Queen of the Night was weeping for her stolen child.

"It's your mother, isn't it?" I asked.

"I think so, yes," replied the daughter of die Königin der Nacht.

"Do you think there will be any stars tomorrow?"

Without hesitation, she nodded.

"There will always be stars. There must be, just as there must be a sunrise. It is for this reason that the Queen of the Night and the Mage of the Day were joined. They cannot be parted, not unless the world itself is."

"But she weeps for you."

"Yes. I believe that she does."

I turned my head to look at her, then, and, for the first time, I saw that she wept also. Not from the eye of gold, the eye she had inherited from her father. That eye was as dry as ashes, and cold ones at that. But from the eye of silver there flowed one tear after another, exactly the same color as the stars in the sky. In so endless a stream I only barely stopped myself from glancing at the hem of my skirt, certain I would find it drenched with the tears that must, by now, have formed a great puddle around us on the floor.

Though they had been separated, they wept together for what had befallen them, the Queen of the Night and her strange-eyed daughter.

"Would she have brought you, do you think?" I asked. "Would she have kept the appointed time?"

The daughter of the Queen of the Night looked down at me, and now I could see that, though the gold eye did not weep, it too was filled with unbearable sorrow.

"I believe she would have," she answered. "For I have never known her to go back on her word, not to anyone. But we'll never know now. The Lord Sarastro has taken care of that."

"He is more than simply the Lord Sarastro," I said. I knew it was foolish, but I couldn't help myself. I had loved him too well, and too long. He had been everything to me. Father and mother both. Yet it seemed to me as if she threw him away, discarded what he was without a thought.

"He is your father."

Even in the dim light, I could see the way hot color flushed her face.

Nicely done, Gayna, I thought. *Who knows what she can do? What power she, herself, controls. If she turns you into a toad, it's no more than you deserve for your stupidity.*

She pulled in a breath as if to speak, then flattened her lips into a thin and unattractive line. At this, I have to say my spirits picked back up a little. I'm only human, and it pleased me to discover that, even for a moment, she could be ugly.

"More your father than mine, I should think," she said. "Is that why you dislike me so much? Not that I would blame you, of course."

Of all the dirty tricks, I thought. She hadn't turned me into a toad after all. Instead, she'd shown me how well I'd done that myself, all on my own.

"Who says that I dislike you?" I asked. "Maybe I do, maybe I don't. Not that I'd need a reason if I do."

This time, I was certain that she smiled, for I could see her face full on.

"Ah, so there is something more," she said. "Let me think." She scrunched her face up in concentration, and it was then I realized that she had stopped crying. I wondered if the sky outside had done the same, but I didn't want to turn my head to look. I didn't want to break our strange tableau.

"There's really only one thing that it can be, of course. The golden boy. Statos."

"He's not a boy," I said hotly as I sat up a little straighter on the stool. "He's a grown man, and the Lord Sarastro's apprentice."

"Is he indeed?" the daughter of the Queen of the Night asked softly. "The Lord Sarastro's *chosen* apprentice?"

"And what if he is?"

"If he is, then he would make a fitting consort for the Lord Sarastro's daughter."

If she'd shot a burning arrow straight into my chest, she couldn't have hit the mark more accurately, nor wounded me more.

"That seems to be the general consensus of opinion," I said, and even I could hear my voice was bitter.

She cocked her head to one side, just like a bird considering which way to pluck a worm from the ground.

"How long have you loved him?"

I opened my mouth to deny it altogether, then shut it with a snap. *Why deny the obvious?* I thought. There were days it seemed to me the whole world must know how I felt about Statos, even Statos himself.

"Do you believe in love at first sight?"

She considered for a moment. "In theory, I do, I suppose. Though not from personal experience. That doesn't quite answer my question, though."

I sighed. "Since I was five. He entered the Lord

Sarastro's household the same year my father was killed."

"The same year the Lord Sarastro took you in to raise as his own," the Lady Mina said, her tone thoughtful. And I realized with a start of horror that I had done the thing I'd sworn I'd never do. I had given her her name in my own mind.

"He raised you," she said again, "as his own daughter. But now he wishes to give the man you love to a total stranger. One who is a daughter by nothing more than a trick of birth. It must be very difficult for you, Gayna. I'm sorry."

"Oh, for pity's sake!" I cried. "Stop it, can't you? Just stop it!"

I shot to my feet, unable to stay still a moment longer. I took several agitated paces away, then whirled back.

"Why can't you just be mean and nasty and ugly? Why must you be understanding and long-suffering? I liked you a lot better when you ranted and raved. It was much easier to dislike you. And nobody said that you could call me by my name."

I stopped, panting just a little, and we stared at each other. I half expected her to get to her feet as well. It's what I would have done. Even the playing field so that we could really go at it. Look each other in the face, stare each other down, eye to eye.

But she did not. Instead, she continued to sit in her chair, her hands folded in her lap.

"You liked me better when it was easier to dislike me?"

"Don't you dare make fun of me," I said, abruptly all too aware of how ridiculous I'd just sounded. I could feel the laughter swarming up the back of my throat. The trouble with being angry is that it not only makes you feel stupid, it encourages you to say stupid things as well. Stupid things that are hard to take back and impossible to erase. And suddenly, there you are.

"I wouldn't," she said. "I mean, I'm not. I always sort of envied you, if it makes you feel any better."

"Envied me," I echoed. "What for?"

"Because you had two fathers," the Lady Mina said simply. "Yours, and mine, even though you didn't get to know yours very well. Whereas I, for all the attention he paid to me, had none."

"You had your mother," I said.

She nodded. "True enough. That was another reason I sometimes envied you. You look much more like her than I."

I stared at her, appalled. All my life I had heard tales of die Königin der Nacht, and none of them good.

"What do you mean?" I asked. "I don't."

"But you do," the Lady Mina said simply. "You have dark hair, as she does. Skin so pale you can almost see right through it. You could be her daughter, except for the eyes."

"Well, but your hair is dark," I said. I was sounding

ridiculous again and I knew it, but it was genuinely the first thing that came to mind.

"You think so?"

At this, she reached up and, with two quick motions, untied and pulled the dark scarf from around her head. Her hair came spilling down around her shoulders.

I think I must have made some sound. To this day, I still don't quite know why I didn't raise a hand to protect my eyes. The only reason I can come up with is that I didn't want to look away. As if, even as my mind went completely blank, it knew this was as close as I would ever come to gazing straight into the rising sun, for that's exactly what color her hair was. Streaming over her shoulders in just the same way the sun spills over the horizon.

"You are beautiful," I said simply. "Why doesn't that make me hate you even more? It certainly ought to, don't you think?"

"Only if what you felt was truly hate to begin with," the Lady Mina replied.

"You're doing it again," I said. "Sounding all sensible and like you know everything. Statos isn't going to like that, you know."

She did rise to her feet at this, the dark scarf falling from her lap, and all that mass of golden hair tumbling down, down, down, until it almost reached the floor.

"I don't care what Statos likes or doesn't like," she said, her tone forceful. "I don't want him, Gayna. I don't want anything the Lord Sarastro has to give. I don't want to take anything from you."

I pulled in a breath. "Do you not even want a father?"

Absolute silence filled the room, more complete than when the Lord and Statos had departed.

"Yes," the Lady Mina said at last. "Yes, of course I want a father. One who sees me for what I am, or wishes to, at the very least. For only then may he see what I may become. I don't want a father who steals me away in the middle of the night. Who breaks his word. Who sees me only as a pawn in some gigantic cosmic game of one-upmanship against my mother.

"Do you think the Lord Sarastro can be that kind of father?"

He has been a good one to me, I thought. But all my life I had known that I was not the Lady Mina, not the Lord Sarastro's true blood daughter, and so I remained silent.

"I'm not so sure I think so either," the Lady Mina said, taking my silence for assent to her view that the Lord Sarastro could not be the father that she wanted. "As he's the only one I've got, it seems simplest not to want him at all."

"You will be very lonely here, then," I said, then bit my tongue. "I'm sorry. Perhaps I should have offered words of comfort."

"No," the Lady Mina said with a quick shake of her head that had her golden hair rippling like the flames of the fire. "Not if they were false. I'd rather know the truth, however unpleasant."

"Even in that case, I really hate to tell you this," I said. "But I think it's nearly dawn. The sky is that funny color that isn't a color. Do you know what I mean?"

"Yes," Mina answered as she turned to look over her shoulder. "I have seen the dawn. There is a moment when the sky goes blank, as if the world is trying to remember what it looks like in the light."

"That's it exactly," I said as I moved to stand at her side. She turned, and together we stood for a moment, gazing out the window. "You should get dressed," I went on finally. "The Lord Sarastro will send for you soon."

"I should be well dressed when I go to be sacrificed? Why should I do anything to please him? Answer me that."

"Then don't do it to please him," I said at once. "Do it to please yourself, and do it for your mother. You speak brave words. Now match it with brave deeds. Show them what the daughter of die Königin der Nacht is made of."

At this, to my complete astonishment, she threw back her head and laughed. "Now you're appealing to my vanity," she said. "That is well done. All right, show me this finery."

"This doesn't mean we're friends, you know," I said as I moved to a wardrobe tucked into an alcove on the far side of the fireplace and flung it open.

"Of course it doesn't," the Lady Mina said, her tone calm. "I think I'm sorry for that. It would be nice to have a friend. I never really had one other than Lapin."

"Lapin?"

She shook her head, as if sorry that she'd spoken. "Not now," she said. "Perhaps another time. What do you think of this one?" she asked. And she pulled from the wardrobe exactly the dress I would have chosen had I been in her place, one made of cloth of beaten gold. "If the Lord Sarastro wishes me to make an impression on his subjects, this ought to do the trick."

Without thinking, I said, "You'll be absolutely blinding."

She laughed again, but it seemed to me there was sadness in the sound. "My thought precisely," she said, and she carried the dress over to the bed and laid it out. "Who knows? Perhaps, while they're hiding their eyes at the mere sight of me, I can make good my escape."

I felt the breath back up inside my lungs. "You would do that? You would try to run?"

She turned her head, then, and those strange eyes looked straight into mine. I'm pretty sure that's when it happened. A single thought, the same thought, appearing simultaneously in two different minds.

"I would," the Lady Mina said as she straightened

slowly. "But I could not do it on my own. The dwelling of the Lord Sarastro is large, and I do not know my way through it. Help would most definitely be required."

"And if you had it?" I asked.

"Then I would go and not look back," the Lady Mina said. "Particularly not at any man with golden hair and bright blue eyes."

"I will help you," I said.

By way of answer, the Lady Mina smiled.

At the sight of it, I felt my heart skip a beat inside my chest even as my determination strengthened. *Statos must never see that smile,* I thought. If he did, he would never look at me again, not that he looked at me all that often now.

"But we must hurry," I said, and I moved toward her. "The sun is nearly up. The lord will send for you at any moment."

To my astonishment, she laughed, as if the danger only added pleasure to the challenge.

"I have an idea to buy us a little more time," the Lady Mina said. "Give me your cloak, and I will give you mine." Then she leaned down and swept up the golden dress, holding it against me. "Let us see how well you look in this finery, shall we?"

The Outsider

I'll never forget my first sight of the Lord Sarastro's daughter, standing fearful yet uncowed at her mother's side. Nor my second one, for that matter, standing motionless and alone in her father's great entry hall. Did not die Königin der Nacht say three times that the Lord Sarastro would regret his actions in stealing their daughter away? And did she not say that the third time pays for all?

Well, I say this. That lady knows what she is talking about.

I cannot say for certain whether the Lord Sarastro came to regret the actions he performed. It is a thing of which we never spoke. But I do know my third sight of the Lady Mina was the one that sealed my fate, assuming it hadn't been sealed already, long before. Standing in the room her father had prepared for her, the hood of her cloak at long last pushed back, I could see her face clearly for the very first time.

This is the picture of her that has never left me, the one that beats with my heart, runs with my blood, holds up my body right along with my bones.

It will stay in my mind until my brain itself becomes as blank as a sheet of new-made parchment, a thing that will mean my heart has stopped.

The simplest way of saying it is this: Even in her pain and defiance, the Lady Mina was beautiful. So beautiful she outshone the moon and the stars alike. Had it been in the sky at the time, I have no doubt she would have outshone the very sun.

The fourth time I saw her, she wasn't the Lady Mina at all.

It was shortly before dawn when the Lord Sarastro summoned me to his study. I was ready, had been for hours. The truth is, I hadn't gone to bed at all. How could I sleep when I knew that everything I'd worked so long and hard for could, should, *would* be mine with the rising of this single sun?

"Ah, Statos, good. Come in," the Lord Sarastro said when I had been ushered in. The servant who had summoned me bowed and departed, leaving me alone with my lord. My lord and master, I probably should say. For, as his apprentice, my master is precisely what the Lord Sarastro was.

I know several of the others have told you their life histories, or something of them. Have no fear that I will follow their example, for I have no intention of boring you to tears with the many details of my life until this moment. For one thing, my life isn't all that unusual or uncommon.

Like many a younger son of parents rich and poor

alike, I was sent to join the Lord Sarastro's household as a boy, in the hope that I might prove worthy enough to join his order. This I did, and in time achieved an unlooked-for honor. I became his chosen apprentice, the one above all others to whom he revealed his thoughts.

None of which may make much difference to you, of course. For I have not forgotten that your first glimpse of me was through the Lady Mina's eyes. Don't think I don't know what that makes me: the villain of this story. I will say this much, though, and suggest that you remember it as you read along.

My desires were, are, no different from the others'. All I wanted was precisely what they did: a place to call my own, a home, and a heart to share it with, to beat in time to mine. And if I did not always do quite what you would have done to accomplish these ends, let me ask you this: How far would *you* go to achieve your heart's desire? If it was almost within your grasp and about to be snatched away, how much farther would you go?

"You conducted yourself very well last night," the Lord Sarastro said, and he gestured me to take a seat while he stayed beside the window. "You made me very proud. I am sure that, with the coming of the sun, my daughter will see reason."

I bowed my head, acknowledging his compliment which pleased me greatly, and showing that I agreed with him when, in fact, I did not. I was far from believing that the Lady Mina would change her opinion of what had happened to her simply because the sun was about to come up. That was nothing new, after all.

And I think that this was the moment I first began to feel afraid. For, if the Lord Sarastro did not see the situation clearly, truly, then the fact that I was the one he had chosen for his daughter would make no difference. All might still be lost. But I did not speak my fears aloud. If there's one thing an apprentice should never do, particularly one attached to a magician so powerful he is literally the living embodiment of the sun, it's to let his master know that he has doubts about his judgment.

"This morning, Mina will be presented to my subjects," the Lord Sarastro continued, by which he mostly meant the members of his court, other magicians of our order, and the people of the nearest town. The lord looks after too many people for them all to be assembled in one place at once, even on so momentous an occasion as this.

"After she has been made known to them, I will present you as her future husband. Then, in the grove most sacred to our order, the ceremony will take place at once.

"Do you not think—," I blurted out, before I could prevent it. I stopped and bit my tongue. Hadn't I just finished promising myself I wouldn't speak my fears?

"What?" the Lord Sarastro asked as he came to sit beside me. "Don't be afraid. Speak what is in your mind."

"Might it not be better to wait?" I asked. "To present me as your daughter's intended husband?"

Give her more time, I wanted to cry. *Time for her to get to know me. Time for me to win her heart. You have control over her body. You've certainly proved that much. But do you think that's all* I *want?*

"If she makes a public denial, her pride may make it difficult for her to take it back," I went on.

This was a thing I knew the Lord Sarastro understood: the power of pride. It had ruled his dealings with his own wife for many a long year.

At my words, the Lord Sarastro's eyebrows winged up, and I felt my stomach clench. Though I had not spoken all I might have wished, still, I had never contradicted him even this much before.

"That is well thought of," he said after a moment's pause. "For she will certainly have pride, if she is anything like her mother."

He rose and returned to his former position, gazing out the window. Had he stood at his window all night, I wondered, as I had at mine? Had he watched as the night tore itself apart in grief, and all in perfect silence? How had he felt to know he was the cause?

"I will not be governed by the pride of a sixteen-year-old girl," the Lord Sarastro said at last. "Particularly not my own daughter. She is subject to my will, as are all who dwell within my lands. The sooner she is made to acknowledge this, the better. Therefore, all shall proceed as I have already spoken."

At this, I rose also and made a bow.

"It shall be as you wish, my lord."

"Indeed," the Lord Sarastro said. "Indeed it shall. Now go. Take those who are without and bring my daughter to the audience hall, Statos. The sun is about to rise."

And so I made my way to the Lady Mina's chamber, the Lord Sarastro's servants following the proper distance behind. Was I proud of myself as I walked along? As every step I took brought me closer to my desire, did I celebrate the fact that, in spite of what her own wishes might be, in a few moments more, the Lady Mina would be made to bow to her father's will, and therefore, to mine?

Surely, the answer must be yes if I am truly the villain you'd like to think I am.

And so it pains me to tell you the truth. Mostly, I concentrated on trying to control my heart, which was suddenly beating high and fast, prancing inside my chest like a racehorse. I tried to figure out if it were possible to wipe my palms upon my pocket handkerchief without the Lord Sarastro's servants noticing, for my hands were clammy and had begun to sweat.

I wondered if I might simply throw up.

I'm sorry if this destroys the image you have of me as a villain, but it is you who have cast me in that role. It is not one I took on for myself. And so, step by painful step, I made my way to the Lady Mina's door.

Upon reaching it, I stopped, pulled in a breath, then nodded for one of the lord's retainers to knock and announce me. The Lord Sarastro is strict on matters of protocol. I was here as his emissary, his representative, and should therefore be accorded the same respect that he would be due.

There was a moment's silence following the servant's brisk knock. Then, "Enter," called a high, clear voice. The servant opened the door and threw it back. I advanced into the room, making a sign that the retainers should close the door behind me, then wait in the corridor.

I had no idea what to expect from the Lady Mina this morning. Was it possible, as her father maintained, that she would come to accept her new situation in just a single night? She was standing with her back to the room, gazing out the great bank of windows, swathed in her great, dark cloak. Even the hood was pulled up over her head. Of Gayna, I could see no sign.

At the click of the door closing fast, the Lady Mina made a small movement, and I could see a flash of gold fabric beneath the cloak's hem.

That is a good sign, I thought. She would not defy

her father completely, for she had dressed to attend the audience.

"Sarastro, Mage of the Day, sends you greetings, Lady Mina," I said. "He welcomes you to your first dawn, and requests that you accompany me to the audience scheduled in your honor."

"My first dawn as his subject, you mean," the Lady Mina said, her voice subdued, muffled by the hood of her cloak. Still, she did not turn around.

"He seeks only to honor you," I said, wishing I didn't feel, and sound, quite so stupid. Wishing I could throw protocol aside and say what I truly wanted.

"And to honor you, as well," the Lady Mina said. "For does he not intend that I shall be your bride? Come now, tell me the truth, Statos."

"That is the lord's desire," I said, choosing my words carefully. "And mine, above all else."

"Truly?" the Lady Mina asked. Again she moved. And again I caught a sudden flash of gold. "More than anything else in the world, you wish to be my husband?"

"I do, Lady," I said.

At this, at long last, the Lady Mina turned around, pushing her cloak back from her face as she did so. At her gesture, I felt the very blood inside my veins congeal.

"And now, Statos?"

"Gayna," I said, my voice no more than a whisper. "For the love of heaven, what have you done?"

What Sometimes Happens to the Best-Laid Plans

(A THING YOU MAY NOT NEED TO BE TOLD)

"What I had to do," I answered, my tone impassioned. "What any subject who truly holds the Lord Sarastro in her heart would have done."

"You helped her get away."

"Yes," I said simply. What was the sense in denying what I had done?

I watched as Statos moved to the chair in front of the now cold fireplace, his movements slow yet jerky, and sat down upon one arm. I have seen men, competitors in the tournaments the Lord Sarastro sometimes hosts, move like this sometimes, when they have taken a blow which does no lasting injury but confuses all the body, the mind most of all.

Then he looked up, his blue eyes dazed, and spoke a single word:

"Why?"

"To show the Lord Sarastro the truth about his daughter's heart," I said. "To prove that she will never bend her will to his, for she does not love him. She does not love you. She is the lord's daughter by blood, but this does not make her worthy of either of you. Forget her, Statos."

To my astonishment, he laughed, and the sound was so bitter it made my throat close up.

"Forget her," he echoed. "Why do you not simply suggest I forget my whole life? Merciful sun in the sky!" he exclaimed as he shot to his feet and began to pace around the room. "How shall I tell the Lord Sarastro of this? You have no idea of the trouble this brings down upon us."

"Then perhaps you'd better tell me," I said. "It would be nice if someone explained something."

He swung around to face me, pivoting swiftly on one heel. His eyes moved over my face for what seemed a lifetime. Long enough for me to feel myself color, then grow pale beneath his scrutiny. For me to feel first hope, then fear take hold of my heart.

"You really don't know, do you?" he finally said quietly. There was in his voice a thing that I had never heard there before, though this is not the same as saying I did not recognize it for what it was.

No, oh no, I thought.

For the thing in his voice sounded remarkably like pity. And, much more than hate, it is pity which is the opposite, the doom, of love. For to love or hate truly, you need to be equals, or at least close in strength. But pity is a thing which flows from the strong to the weak. From the *haves* to the *have-nots.*

"Know what?" I asked, though the truth was, I

was far from certain that I wanted to know.

"There is a reason the Lord Sarastro did not take his daughter into his household before now. A prophecy was made in the hour of her birth."

"A prophecy," I said. "I suppose I should have known. Wait a minute. Don't tell me." I raised a hand as I saw him take a breath to go on. "It doesn't just concern the Lord Sarastro's daughter. It also concerns her husband."

"That is so," Statos replied. He began to move about the room again, though not with the agitation he had showed before. This was the way he moved when he was thinking something through, trying to come up with an explanation for a difficult problem. A thing he did without being aware he was doing it, and one of the things I loved most about him.

"According to the prophecy, when the Lady Mina weds, the very world itself will change," he said softly now. "And the powers of her parents, of the Night and the Day, will also change. They will at once grow weaker and more strong."

In spite of myself, I gave a snort. "Just once, I'd like to hear a simple, straightforward prophecy."

Statos gave a bark of surprised laughter. For a moment, I saw genuine amusement and appreciation light in his cobalt eyes. I felt a clutch inside my chest.

How much easier my life would be if I did not love you! I thought. *How much less painful, but how much plainer. How much less color there would be in the world.*

"Who comes up with such things, anyhow?"

"I don't have the faintest idea," Statos replied. "The powers that watch over the universe, I assume."

"And they're interested in the Lady Mina and whom she might marry."

He nodded, and the smile faded from his eyes.

"It seems that they are. The Lord Sarastro's interest is only natural, of course. He has devoted the Lady Mina's lifetime to finding the true meaning of the prophecy. Since it tells that the world will be altered not by the birth of a daughter but by her marriage, the lord has reasoned that the key lies in finding the right husband for her.

"But he hardly saw her until yesterday," I protested. "How can he find her the right husband when he doesn't even know her?"

"He does not need to know her," Statos said, both his tone and his expression betraying his surprise at my agitation over what he considered to be obvious. "In fact, he does not wish to."

I think my mouth actually dropped open. I loved the Lord Sarastro, and I had trusted him since I was a small child. But there are some things that simply don't make sense.

"Don't be ridiculous," I said. "Of course he needs to know her. How else can he find the proper husband?"

"By reason," Statos said simply. "Reason and nothing more. This is why, much as he sometimes mistrusts her, he gave the raising of Mina over to her mother, the Queen of the Night. The Lord Sarastro feared that, if he raised his daughter himself, if he watched her grow as other fathers do . . ."

"It might be difficult for him to deny her if her choice was different from his own," I filled in softly.

"That is it, precisely," answered Statos. "He could not afford to run the risk that he would be swayed by his, or the Lady Mina's emotions. More than her happiness is at stake in this. There is the fate of the world itself."

"To say nothing of the fate of his own power," I said suddenly, and I think it's fair to say that I surprised us both. This was as close as I had ever come to criticizing the Lord Sarastro. "The prophecy says only that the Lady Mina's parents will each grow weaker and stronger upon her marriage. It doesn't say in what proportion."

Statos nodded, his expression thoughtful. "That is true also. Therefore, the lord reasoned that the best choice for his daughter would be a member of his own order. Someone he knew he could trust absolutely, for he had helped to guide his steps himself."

"You," I said. "His favorite, his chosen apprentice. How well everything works out."

"The Lord Sarastro has a reason for everything he does," Statos said simply. "It is his way, the way of our order."

"Why did he choose to raise me, I wonder?"

Then, even as I posed the question, a reason occurred to me. One my mind informed me just might break what was left of my already-battered heart.

"But surely you know the answer to that," Statos said.

"So that he could know what a young girl was like," I said, and I thought my own words might suffocate me. "To raise a girl without actually having to raise his own daughter. I am a stand-in. An experiment. A cipher."

"Of course not," Statos said at once. He moved to where I stood, turned me to face him, and grasped me by the upper arms. "He honored your parents, especially your father, Gayna. Raising you simply shows his respect."

I felt a dreadful impulse to laugh and fought it down.

"Respect," I said, and I looked up into those blue, blue eyes. "Honor. Those are fine words, Statos. But for all they speak of noble things, they come from the mind and not the heart. So tell me, what of love? Does the Lord Sarastro love me? Do *you*? *Can* you even love?"

I felt his hands flex, involuntarily, upon my arms.

"Gayna," he said. "I-it does no good to ask such questions. They can change nothing."

"My lord!" A brisk knock sounded on the chamber

door. At the sound, Statos started, his grip tightening yet again. "The hour grows late."

"Merciful heavens!" Statos whispered. "The Lord Sarastro's audience. How can I tell him that his daughter has run away rather than bend her will to his?"

"Let me tell him," I said, though the very words brought despair to my heart. "It is I who should bear the brunt of his displeasure, not you, for I showed her the way out."

"No," Statos said at once. And now, at last, he let me go. "I will tell him. I will do my duty."

He turned toward the door.

"Just tell me one thing," I said, and, at the sound of my voice, he stopped, though he did not turn around. "I have no idea what's going to happen next, but I don't imagine it's going to be very pleasant for me. Tell me the truth about this one thing before you go to the Lord Sarastro."

"What do you want to know?"

More than anything in the world, I wished to close my eyes, so that I might not have to see his reaction. I kept them open.

"*Could* you have loved me? If there had been no prophecy, if it made no difference whose blood flows in my veins and whose in the Lady Mina's, would she still have been your choice? Or might you have made another?"

"Why do you ask me such things?" Statos said,

and his voice was weary. "Have I not already told you they can change nothing?"

"I'm not asking that anything change," I said. "All I'm asking for is knowledge. You ought to understand that. Knowledge is a thing of the mind. If you had been free to choose, would you still have chosen the Lord Sarastro's daughter?"

"I have always been free to choose, Gayna," Statos said.

Then he went out, and closed the door quietly behind him.

In Which a New Friendship Is Formed

All that night, I played the bells.

I played until my hands went numb to the wrists, and then the elbows, and, finally, the shoulders. Until calluses formed upon my palms, hardened, and then split open. Until the bright blood trickled slowly down my fingers in a never-ending stream, and the bells themselves were colored red and gold. I played until I was beyond hunger, beyond thirst, beyond pain, but still within the bounds of hope.

Just as dawn was breaking, the birds arrived.

Every single bird I'd ever called to me in the course of my life swooped down in a great wheeling mass just as the sun burst over the horizon. Some settled on the ground at my feet in the clearing where I sat. Others lined the branches of the nearby trees. Still others turned in spirals above my head, making a great exclamation point in the lightening sky.

Yet, in spite of these different actions, all had one thing in common. Save for the beating of their wings, not one bird made a sound, as if knowing in their hearts, as I did in mine, that no other voice should be raised. Nothing must come between the ears of the wide world and the call of the bells.

Last to come was the nightingale, who settled into her usual position upon my shoulder, though this was hardly her usual time of day to do so. I knew that she was there only by the quick flash of wings I caught out of the corner of my eye. I think my entire body had gone numb by then. The only parts still functioning were my arms, my hands, and my heart.

My mind felt as thin and blank as a sheet of pounded metal. Not that my mind was really all that important at the moment. The mind is a wonder and can accomplish many things. But it cannot accomplish the impossible. That is a thing only the heart can do, though a strong will helps also.

The impossible began to happen shortly before noon. That's when the young man finally showed up, stumbling into the clearing like a drunkard, then pulling up short. Blinking, as if he couldn't quite trust the sight in his own eyes.

At his arrival, every single bird turned to stare. Those on the ground looked up. Those in the trees looked down. Those still in the air ceased to beat their wings, opened them to glide, and craned their necks. As for me, I continued to play the bells. It had taken a long time for anything to show up, it was true. But there was no guarantee the first thing to show up was going to be the right one.

"I'm here," the young man gasped, and he sounded so out of breath I wondered if he had run the whole way from wherever it was that he had started out. "I'm sorry it took so long. I'm not too late, am I?"

At his words, the stone hammer slipped from my numb fingers and fell upon the ground, and the bright noonday was filled with silence.

"You are not too late," I said. "Who are you?"

"I am called Tern," the young man said. "And I'm a prince, if that's important."

"Tern," I echoed, not quite certain I had heard him right.

He made a face. "It's an unusual name, I know. It's a kind of seabird, to tell you the truth. But my younger brother's name is Arthur."

"How nice for him. I am called Lapin," I said. It was the first time I'd volunteered my name in as long as I could remember. "You don't have to tell me what it means. I already know."

"Your name means something too?" the young man asked, his voice surprised. And at this, three separate things happened, all at once.

I threw back my head and laughed.

The birds opened their throats and began to sing.

And, muffled in a cloak to guard against the light of day, die Königin der Nacht arrived.

And New Plans Are Formed

"Do you know who I am?" she asked.

I felt a wild impulse to laugh and fought it down. It could, quite truthfully, be said I wasn't all that sure I knew anything anymore, though I had managed to find the one who played the bells and produce my own name upon request, both of which I took to be good signs.

Pull yourself together, Tern, I thought. *You are a prince, after all.*

"Madam," I answered, wishing I could say something other than what I was about to. "I regret that I do not. Though please don't take it personally. I seem to be saying, 'I don't know,' an awful lot all of a sudden. Though it might help things if I could see your face."

I watched her turn her head in Lapin's direction, the movement as eloquent as if she'd spoken aloud.

Is this the best that you could do? it asked.

"He said his name was Tern," Lapin offered mildly.

"Did he, indeed?" the woman said, and her head turned back toward me. "Perhaps this will help," she said. And she pushed back the hood of her cloak.

For the span of my swiftly indrawn breath, the world grew still. A great darkness reached out to cover the sun, though there was not a cloud in the sky. And, in that moment, I released my breath, for I thought I knew. She pulled the hood back over her face and the sun shone out once more.

"Well?"

"There are tales in my land," I said, "told mostly to lull children to sleep. Tales of a great queen who watches over the night. She is complicated, the tales say. Like the night, she is many different things at once. Some say she has a voice of silk. Others, that she has a will of iron. But all agree on one thing: Her beauty has no equal."

"Just one," answered the Queen of the Night. "My daughter. Will you look upon her likeness?"

"If it pleases you," I said.

"Oh, for crying out loud," Lapin suddenly exclaimed. "I didn't play the bells until my fingers bled just so the two of you could sound like you're in the middle of a court audience. We haven't got a lot of time here, in case you've forgotten. Can't you just tell him what needs to be done and get on with it? Some of us haven't had much rest and are tired."

I half expected her to strike him dead for his impertinence right on the spot, always assuming she actually had the power to do so. Instead the Queen of the Night simply smiled.

"You'll have to forgive Lapin," she said calmly. "He can be annoying, especially when he's right and he knows it."

"There's something you need me to do?" I asked. Perhaps all of this was about to make sense.

"Why did you come here, young Tern?" she asked by way of a reply.

"Because I had to," I said simply. "The bells didn't give me any choice."

"Bells," said the Queen of the Night.

I nodded. "I heard bells," I said. "And it seemed to me that they called to me. More than that, their call was a summons."

"And so you answered it, just like that?"

"Not precisely," I acknowledged. "I don't know how things are where you live, Lady, but, where I come from, knowing your heart and what it holds is considered pretty important."

The Queen of the Night took another step toward me, so close that, if I had dared, I could have reached out and touched her.

"Did the call of the bells match what is in your heart, young Tern?"

"No," I answered truthfully. "Not precisely. But it was as close as anything has ever come. Too close a match to be ignored, even if I had wanted to. And so I came. It's as simple as that. What does it mean? Do you know?"

"I do," said the Queen of the Night. "But answer

me just one more question first. What color are your eyes?"

It would have to be that, I thought.

"That is a question not even my mother can answer, not to her own satisfaction, anyway," I replied. "For I am told that my eyes change color according to the light.

"In the morning, they are golden. At midday, green. By late afternoon, they have mellowed to fawn brown. My brother, Arthur, insists that they turn gray as a pewter plate at twilight, then silver when the first stars appear in the sky. At full night, things are easier for all concerned, for, at a certain point, I simply close my eyes. My father calls them hazel, and says we should simply leave it at that.

"My hair is just plain brown," I added after a brief pause.

The Queen of the Night smiled. "There is nothing plain about you, young Tern," she said. She looked over her shoulder at Lapin. "Let your heart rejoice, for you have done well."

At this, Lapin got to his feet and swept her a tired bow, a thing that made the birds around him eddy like leaves in a gentle wind.

"My heart can never truly rejoice until the Lady Mina's does."

"Well spoken," the Queen of the Night said, and she turned back to me. "Come walk with me, Tern, and I will tell you what you need to know."

❖❖ ❖❖ ❖❖

"I have a daughter," the Queen of the Night said. "Mina, my only child. Last night, she was stolen from me by a mighty sorcerer, the Lord Sarastro, who intends to choose a husband for her. Unfortunately, he's also her father."

That would be the night of the storm, I thought. *The night the world began to change.*

"I would have my daughter set free," the Queen of the Night continued. "But more than that, I wish her to have the freedom to know, and choose, from her own heart. While her father holds her, this can never happen, for he would have her bend her will to his."

"But—," I said.

The Queen held up a hand for silence.

"I know what you will say," she pronounced. "That many a father has chosen a daughter's husband. The fact that this is true has never made it right. But more than this, Mina's father broke an oath when he took her from me. I cannot trust him to do what is right for our daughter.

"Therefore, Mina must be set free, and so I set Lapin to play the bells."

"Wishing your daughter to be freed from captivity I understand," I said. "But I don't understand about the bells."

"The bells have been in Lapin's family since his grandmother's time," the Queen said. "They were a gift from the powers that watch over the universe. If struck correctly, they enable the player to summon their true love to their side."

"I don't think Lapin is my true love," I said.

"I'm pleased to hear it," the Queen of the Night answered with a smile. "But I set Lapin a special task, to play the bells in a way they had never been played before. He has known my daughter since she was an infant. It was his hopes for her that he held in his heart when he played the bells, not his hopes for himself. And this was the hope that I held in mine:

"That Lapin's playing would call to the one who could both rescue my daughter and win her heart, for the call of the bells would come so close to the music of his own heart that he could not refuse to answer its summons."

"Oh," I said. It was a pretty accurate description of what I'd experienced, I had to admit.

At this, the Queen of the Night gave a laugh as silver as her eyes. "Come," she said, and she reached inside her cloak and drew out a locket made of silver. "Let me show you my daughter's likeness."

"It doesn't matter what she looks like," I said swiftly. "Not if she is the true match of my heart. And even if it turns out that she isn't, she's been wronged and needs to be rescued. I can certainly do that much."

She paused then, with the hand that held the locket half-extended toward me. "I do believe you are afraid, young Tern."

"Well, of course I'm afraid," I said.

"Of what?"

"Of every part of this," I answered, seeing no reason not to be completely honest. "It's changed my whole life. I'd be foolish not to be afraid, I think. But that doesn't mean I won't do what needs to be done."

"Perhaps your whole life has been spent in waiting for this moment and you just didn't know it," the Queen suggested. "In which case, all you are doing is fulfilling your destiny and not changing anything at all."

"Perhaps," I acknowledged.

"All right. Let's say you end up rescuing my daughter, but nothing more," she said. "Not that that wouldn't be quite a lot. It would still be helpful to know what she looks like, don't you think?"

"You'll have to excuse me for being an idiot," I said. "I think I've been up as long as Lapin has, for, as long as he played, I listened."

The Queen of the Night threw back her head and laughed once more. Then she sobered, and those eyes like stars looked straight into mine.

"When Mina was taken, I was sure I'd never laugh again. Sure that my own heart was broken. I think you will do very well, young Tern. Now take this, and look upon my daughter."

I've never really believed in love at first sight, though that could be nothing more than rejecting the notion because it hadn't happened to me, I suppose. And it isn't altogether accurate to say that love at first sight is what happened to me at that particular moment. Because the truth is, this wasn't my first glimpse of the Lady Mina's face. I had seen it before.

This was the face that my mind had been conjuring, slowly yet surely, ever since I first played the flute that I had carved from the heart of the King's Oak, and heard it answered by a call of bells. Hazy, at first, its features indistinct, growing more and more clear the closer I came to the sound of the bells. Right up until the moment that I had burst into the clearing, at which point the sight of Lapin and all that had happened since had driven the image to the back of my mind.

But not, as it happens, from any portion of my heart. For, at the sight of the face in the locket, my heart gave a great leap, and, after that, all my mind needed was but a small step to understand the cause. It was the Lady Mina's face I had been moving toward, her call I had heard in the voice of the bells. And, as her mother hoped, so, now, did I. That the reason I had been summoned would be because the Lady Mina's heart was the one true match for mine.

"Well?" the Queen of the Night inquired softly. "Will you know my daughter when you see her again?"

"I would know her anywhere," I said. "For her face is written in my heart."

At this, she laid her hand upon my arm. "You give my heart hope, young Tern," she said. "Lapin!"

A moment later, slightly disheveled, as if he had fallen asleep, Lapin appeared in a flurry of birds.

"Did I hear my mistress's voice?"

"There's no need to be cheeky just because you know I'm pleased with you," said the Queen of the Night. "Besides, there's no time to rest on your laurels. I want you to go with Tern."

"He's a prince!" Lapin protested. "They're supposed to be good at this sort of thing. He doesn't need my help."

"He does. Mina knows you, while he is still a stranger. Though not, I hope, for very long."

Lapin gave a great, exaggerated sigh. "Oh, very well. If I must do everything, then I guess I must."

He is making it all up, putting on an act, I thought. *He wishes to go as much as she wishes to send him.*

"I will be glad of your company," I said, and found that I meant it.

"Oh, well, that settles it then," Lapin said, but I thought I detected a twinkle in his tired eyes. "It's not every day I get to be a sidekick to a prince."

"Enough!" said the Queen of the Night. "Let my women tend to your hands, Lapin. Then you and Tern should set out at once."

"Which way shall we go?" I asked. For, now that I didn't have the call of the bells to guide me, I realized I wasn't quite sure precisely where I was, let alone where the path by which I had arrived had gone.

"Lapin knows the way," replied the Queen of the Night. "I have done all that I dare. Now it is up to you."

In Which Many Things Begin to Converge

THOUGH THIS MAY TAKE MORE THAN A SINGLE CHAPTER TO ACCOMPLISH

It seemed like such a splendid idea, at the time.

To run away, and thereby escape from the Lord Sarastro and show my defiance of him, both at once. And not only that, to run away just at dawn. At the moment when the sun begins to reclaim its ownership of the world, just as the lord wished to claim ownership over me.

Could there have been a more complete rejection of his plans for me, of all he stood for? I thought not. Oh, yes, it was a brave and splendid idea, one worthy of a heroine in an adventure novel. One who was going to have a happy ending beyond her wildest dreams.

Eventually.

In the meantime, she—I—was being forced to admit a painful truth.

Running away really isn't all that much fun.

In the first place, the tunnels through which I was making my escape were dark. Not a problem for me, or so you and I would both have thought. But the darkness of the hidden passageway through which I moved was not the kind to which I was accustomed. It was close and cold. The further I moved along it, the more it seemed to me that I was walking through my own tomb.

Gayna had discovered the series of passages as a child, she had told me as we raced to put our spontaneously made plans into effect. Though the Lord Sarastro had taken her in, there were few women in his household. As a result, Gayna was often left unattended for long periods of time. Like any child, she'd been eager to explore, and, consequently, she had discovered a series of narrow passages that seemed to her to run between the very walls of the Lord Sarastro's dwelling.

What this meant, what their purpose was, Gayna had never learned, for she had never confided her discovery to anyone. As she had grown older and her household duties had increased, she'd visited the tunnels less and less frequently, but she had never forgotten them. There was an entrance to one behind the wardrobe in the room in which I'd spent the night. And it was through this passage that Gayna proposed I make my escape, while she, dressed in the finery intended for me, would stay behind.

"Stick to the main passageway," Gayna had said as she bundled me into her own cloak. "This should be easy, for it is wider than the others. Turn neither to the left nor to the right. Keep walking until you come to a great stone door. If you put your two hands together in the center and push with all your might, the door will open. You must then hurry through it quickly, for, as soon as you have let it go, it will swing back all on its own. I don't know how it does this, but I do know it's heavy enough to crush you."

"I will take care," I said.

We stood back and regarded one another. She was beautiful in the fancy dress we'd found, its gold a perfect complement to her dark hair and her fine, pale skin.

"He's a fool not to want you," I said, then cursed *myself* for a fool when I saw her cheeks flush and the tears rise, unwanted, in her eyes. "But perhaps he does, and cannot show it," I hurried on. "The Lord Sarastro is his master, after all. And if he has other plans for Statos—"

"Perhaps," Gayna interrupted. "And perhaps I'll ask him and see what he does. But as for you, you'd better go. There isn't much time. It's nearly dawn."

Moving past me, she fiddled with the back of the wardrobe. I heard a click, then watched as Gayna put her hands in the center of the back of the wardrobe and pushed. It swung back, and a draft of cold and musty air poured out. Gayna stayed where she was, her weight against the door. Beyond her, I couldn't see a single thing.

"Thank you for everything, Gayna," I said. "Good luck."

"And to you," the girl my father had raised instead of me said.

Then I stepped forward into the passage. She stepped back. And the door swung closed behind me.

"Do you actually know where we're going?" I asked. "Not that I'm complaining or anything. But we have been walking for several hours."

Lapin yawned hugely, a thing he had been doing off and on ever since we'd started out. I couldn't precisely blame him, but it was starting to get on my nerves. It's not exactly as if I'd had any more sleep than he had, after all.

"Of course I know where we're going," he said now. "I'm just being careful, taking the long way around. We can hardly march right up to Sarastro's front gates, pound on the door, and demand that he let the Lady Mina go."

"Oh, I don't know," I said after a moment. "He and all his retainers might die laughing. Then we could walk right in."

There was a moment of silence. Then Lapin gave a chuckle, a pleasing sound. All the more pleasant because it seemed to have put an end to the yawning.

"You will be a worthy adversary for the Lord Sarastro," he said. "I don't think he'll be expecting a sense of humor, somehow."

"What will he be expecting?" I asked. A question that had been much on my mind.

"I'm not sure, to tell you the truth," Lapin acknowledged. He gave a grunt of exertion as, together, we scrambled up a series of boulders.

We had been climbing steadily since we started out, as if the course Lapin had set would take us to the very top of the mountain. The slope had been gentle, at first, the forest dense all around us. As we climbed higher, the land began to change. The trees thinned and the ground grew rocky.

"He may not be expecting anyone at all," Lapin continued, pausing for a moment to catch his breath. "I don't think anyone's ever truly challenged the Lord Sarastro's authority before."

"Not even your mistress?" I asked, then bit my tongue. I have a tendency to speak before I think, a trait which I know often worried my father, for it's the kind of thing that can get a person into serious trouble.

"Actually," Lapin said, "they stay out of one another's way as much as possible. Not that this has prevented either from feeling threatened, if you know what I mean."

I thought I did. "Oh," I said after a moment.

"Precisely," Lapin commented. "And now, young prince, if you are rested, we'd better keep going. I'm thinking standing on the top of these rocks leaves us too exposed to prying eyes."

With that, he began to clamber down.

"Wait just a minute," I said as I followed. "We stopped so *you* could rest, not I."

"You just go right on believing that," Lapin suggested.

In the air above us, I heard a single bird call, sounding as if it were laughing at us both.

"Gone," the Lord Sarastro said. "What do you mean my daughter is gone?"

"She isn't in her room, my lord. It would appear that she has run away."

There, I thought. *I've done it.*

I'd told my lord and master that his daughter had fled rather than be subject to his will. Rather than be my wife. Now all I had to do was to wait for the explosion. The only bright spot about the situation that I could see was that I'd been able to reach the Lord Sarastro before he'd entered his great audience hall. He'd still been in his antechamber, and this meeting between us was, therefore, private. I'd stationed the retainers who had accompanied me to the Lady Mina's chamber outside the door to help make sure of that fact.

"Run away! Impossible!" the Lord Sarastro exclaimed now. "She would not dare. She is still my daughter."

"She *is* your daughter, my lord," I replied. "It would seem that this means many things, including that she will dare much."

At this, the Lord Sarastro stopped, and his face grew hard. "She is her mother's daughter also," he said. "Surely the Queen of the Night has had some hand in this. I should never have left my daughter alone, Statos. I should have married her to you at once."

I'm not so sure that would have made a difference, I thought. Not to the Lady Mina's desire to escape, at any rate. Though it might have deprived her of the means.

I must tell him how it happened, I thought. *I must do my duty.* But I discovered I was filled with a strange reluctance. Try as I might, I couldn't shake the image of Gayna from my mind. Gayna, who had grown up here as an outsider, just as I had. Who longed for many things, just as I did. But longed, most of all, to be loved.

Just do it and get it over with, I told myself. *You can't afford to think of Gayna now.*

I drew a breath to speak, but the Lord Sarastro suddenly spoke before I could.

"But I didn't leave her alone, did I?" he asked, his tone quiet, almost as if he was speaking to himself and not to me at all. "I feared she might be lonely, and so I did not leave her on her own. I left Gayna with her, did I not, Statos?"

Now I did find my voice. "You did, my lord."

"My daughter is unfamiliar with my dwelling," the Lord Sarastro continued, "for she never set foot in it before last night. She could not have run away all on her own. I did not aid her, and I'm certain you did not. To do so would destroy both our hopes. In fact, I can think of only one member of my household who might have wished my daughter elsewhere."

He moved to the door and yanked it open.

"Bring Gayna to me at once."

There are many fine sayings in the world. This one, for instance: *The darkest hour is just before the dawn.*

Not true. I can tell you this from personal experience. For on the morning that I helped the Lady Mina run away, it was the hours before the dawn that had been filled with the brilliance of hope. Despair didn't set in until the sun came up, for, with the sun, came Statos.

He did not love me. Not because he couldn't, but because he wouldn't. He was not looking for love alone, as I was. He was looking for his marriage to make him a place in the world, a place no one could take from him. A desire I could understand all too well. A fact which made the situation even worse, somehow. Why could he not see how well matched we were?

All of a sudden, I couldn't stand it anymore. What good did it do me to love? Had I not loved Statos from the first moment I saw him? Loved the Lord Sarastro better than his own flesh and blood? Yet in neither case would my love do me any good, for mine was not the love that was desired. It was as valuable as a counterfeit coin. It would buy me nothing.

There is no reason for me to stay here, I thought. I could see the future, and it was bitter and bleak.

Moving quickly, my body in motion before my mind could contradict, I walked across the room, untying the Lady Mina's cloak and folding it over one arm as I did so. To appear in a cloak might arouse notice. There was no real reason for me to go out, as all were being summoned to the Lord Sarastro's audience that morning. But appearing in the finery I wore beneath would be quite appropriate.

Now all I could do was hope that Statos hadn't posted any men in the hall outside. I pulled in a breath, grasped the knob, twisted it, and pulled open the door.

"What do you mean you cannot find her?" the Lord Sarastro roared.

The retainer swallowed audibly, and I knew a moment of pity. By rights, I should have been the one facing the lord's anger.

"I went to the chamber as you commanded, my lord. But when I knocked, announcing your summons, there was no reply. Three times I called, and still there was no answer. So I opened the door and went inside. The Lady Gayna is not in her room. She is nowhere in your dwelling that I can discover."

The Lord Sarastro gave a bark of unamused laughter. "It seems we have an epidemic of disappearances on our hands, Statos. But those who run would do well to remember they invite others to pursue."

He turned his golden eyes upon me, then, and though the anger was plain to see, it seemed to me there was something else in the Lord Sarastro's eyes. A thing that I had never seen before. And that thing was doubt. Perhaps even fear. For no one had truly set their will against his until this moment.

"Find my daughter, Statos," he said. "Do this yourself. You may dispatch others to search for Gayna."

"My lord, I will," I promised. Though my heart knew a sudden and unexpected pang. Perhaps Gayna had been right to be bitter after all. She would always come second to the Lord Sarastro's blood daughter.

"When you have found her, send word, then take her to the grove most sacred to our order," the lord went on. "There, I shall decide what must be done."

"My lord, I will," I said again. Then I departed in haste, leaving him alone.

Meetings

I walked for what felt like hours, though, as I had no real sense of where I was going, I also had no real way to gauge the time. The passage twisted and turned, sometimes narrowing so abruptly that I had to slide sideways, my back against one wall and my skirts brushing against the one opposite. Eventually, though, it always widened out again, a thing which made me glad. For I discovered that I did not like to be so closely confined.

When it wasn't widening, narrowing, or twisting, the passage climbed until my breath labored and my heart pounded in my head, then plunged so steeply my legs ached walking down the incline. Sweat first gathered, then cooled on my skin, causing me to pull my cloak close around me. But no matter what direction the tunnel took, two things remained constant:

The dust and the dark.

The first was simply an annoyance. I found I was unable to rid myself of the fear that I might sneeze and give myself away, in spite of the thickness of the stone walls with which I was surrounded. Had Gayna not warned it was better not to risk a light?

But, as the moments slipped by and still my journey continued, I discovered a strange thing. One I had never thought to learn.

I discovered how it is that people come to be afraid of the dark.

Until now, the dark had never been an enemy, for it had never been, nor had it contained, anything unknown. Everything about the dark had been comforting and familiar, and so it was little more than a change in my ability to distinguish my surroundings.

But all of that was different now.

Now, for the first time, the darkness brought no comfort, for I did not know what it might hold. And the longer I moved through it, the more uncertain I became. The longer I walked, the more the dark seemed to be a living, breathing entity. A thing with a will that might set it against mine.

Or perhaps it was nothing more sinister than this: In the dark, I began to doubt the course that I had chosen.

What if Gayna has played me false? I wondered. Wouldn't this be the perfect way to get rid of an enemy? To guarantee an escape that led instead to a dead end, no way out, and an endless journey in the dark? Almost at once, I was rewarded for this ungenerous thought by stubbing my toe against the wall.

I leaned for a moment against the passage wall, wiggling my stubbed toe in the air, waiting for the pain to subside.

It does no good to think that way, I chastised myself. *Either she's false or she isn't. And either way, it's too late to worry about it now. You made your choice. All you can do is keep on going. Unless you'd like to go back and give yourself up.*

I tried to imagine what might happen then. Just for an instant, it seemed the Lord Sarastro stood in the passageway beside me, so clearly could I picture his anger in my mind. I could see his golden eyes cloud with it, furious that I had escaped from him in the first place, completely disregarding the fact that I hadn't gotten very far.

"You will be married to Statos right this instant!" the lord would no doubt thunder.

So all my running away would have accomplished would have been to land me right back in the place from which I'd run. Except this time, I'd be married to Statos, and the chains which bound me would be even tighter.

No! I'm not going to let that happen, I thought. I put my foot back down and kept on walking.

Moments later, I found the door. I did this by quite literally walking straight into it, a thing which made me take two staggering steps back and sit down, hard, on the dusty stone floor. It then took me several more moments to determine that it really *was* the door and not simply another wall. But Gayna had told me to continue straight. To turn to neither the left nor to the right. And, as turning was the only way

I could continue, I could reach but one conclusion: At long last, I had come to the way out. Now all I had to do was open the door.

Push in the very center with both hands, Gayna had said. And I remembered that this was the same way she had opened the door in the back of the wardrobe. But it is one thing to find the center of a door when you can see it clearly. It's quite another to do so when you can't see anything at all. So I did the only thing I could. I began to explore the stone with my fingers, hoping to discover the seams that marked the outline of the door.

My fingertips were raw and bleeding before I was through. And, in the end, much to my surprise, I found that I was smiling. For the door was small, shorter than I was. In all likelihood, not much taller than Gayna herself must have been when she'd first come here as a child. In order to push in the very center, I would have to kneel, then crawl out as quickly as I could before the door swung closed. It would probably also help to roll to one side as I did so, the better to prevent my skirts getting caught in the door.

I could just imagine the looks on the faces of the Lord Sarastro's soldiers when they found me, sitting on the ground with my skirts trapped in solid rock.

Stop being foolish, Mina, I scolded myself. *You've come this far. You'll do what needs to be done. Now stop procrastinating and get this over with.*

And so I knelt, put my hands side by side in the

center of the door, and pushed with all my might.

I think that, in spite of Gayna's assurances, I expected some resistance. This couldn't be an exit used very often, after all. But the door gave way so suddenly I tumbled straight out. Then, as it happened, rolling to one side to avoid catching my skirts proved to be a totally unnecessary precaution. The door opened onto a steep slope. My own momentum propelled me forward and out.

For one terrifying moment, I stared straight into open space. Then, after giving one great cry of dismay, I somersaulted down the mountainside.

It was the scream that got our attention. A scream in the forest is pretty hard to ignore. One moment, we'd been climbing silently, yet steadily, our breath moving in and out the only sound. In the next, a great cry split the air, and then there came a great rustling and scraping, as if the top of the mountain lost its hold and was sliding toward the bottom.

"This way," Lapin said, his tone urgent. Together, we began to run. We hadn't covered much ground at all before Lapin stopped so abruptly I ran right into him. The two of us tumbled unceremoniously to the ground.

"Thanks a lot," he whispered as soon as he'd cleared the leaves from his mouth.

"Thanks yourself," I whispered back, hoping I hadn't broken anything useful in the fall. "You might give a fellow a little more warning next time. Why are we whispering, by the way?"

Lapin nodded his head in the direction in which we'd been moving before we'd come to our sudden stop.

"See for yourself."

I looked. "I see what you mean," I said.

"I thought you might."

In front of us, across a rocky space of ground, stood the largest bear I had ever seen, reared up on its hind legs, its muzzle peeled back in a snarl, though it made no sound. A short distance in front of it crouched a cub. And, in between, lying flat and unmoving on its stomach, was a figure with hair as golden as the sun.

"That's the Lady Mina," Lapin whispered.

"I know."

"Well, don't just lie there. Go and rescue her."

"Lapin," I sighed. "I can't go charging in front of that bear any more than we could go knock on Sarastro's front door. We have to be clever. We have to have a plan."

"I'd think of something quickly, if I were you," Lapin said. "I don't think that mother bear is going to give us much time."

"Maybe we can distract it, lure it away," I said. Slowly, I began to ease myself to my feet. But, even as I spoke, I knew such a plan was hopeless. No mother bear alive would leave her cub if she could help it.

No mother bear alive, I thought.

At that moment, as if sensing my intentions, the she-bear swiveled her muzzle toward me, glowering at me with dark brown eyes. And now, at last, she made a sound. A growl in her throat that caused the very marrow in my bones to quiver. I reached for my sword. Yet, even as I drew it, I paused. She was only doing what any mother would. Seeking to protect her child.

"It's a pity my grandmother isn't here," Lapin murmured as he eased to his feet. "She summoned bears when she played the bells, and not one of them growled. But then music soothes the savage beast, or so they say."

"Idiot! Lamebrain! Peahead!" I suddenly exclaimed in a loud voice, a thing that caused the she-bear to give another growl and turn more fully toward us.

"There's no reason to get personal about it," Lapin said.

"I'm talking about myself, not you," I answered. "Here. Hold this."

I thrust the sword in his direction.

"Now wait just a minute!" Lapin protested. "I'm just the sidekick around here, remember? Besides, I'm no good with anything sharp. I always end up cutting something I'm not supposed to, usually some portion of myself."

"I don't want you to use it," I snapped. "I want you

to hold it. I have something with me that may work better than a sword. You were the one who said we didn't have much time. Suppose you just shut up and do as I ask?"

"You're as grouchy as the bear," Lapin complained, but at least he took the sword. Moving quickly now, I reached inside my tunic and brought out the flute that I had carved from the heart of the King's Oak.

"A flute," Lapin said. "You're going to tame a bear with that?"

I pulled in a breath. "I'm going to try."

At that exact moment, the Lady Mina lifted her head. The she-bear swung around. From her throat, there came much more than a growl. She took two menacing steps in the Lady Mina's direction.

"Any time would be just fine, I'm thinking," Lapin said.

I put my lips to the flute and began to play.

I was dreaming. That had to be it. What other explanation could there be for what was going on?

I remembered walking through the dark for an endless amount of time, then light so bright it was blinding. A vicious tumble downhill. And after that, nothing for I had no idea how long. But, at last, my slowly returning senses began to tell me many things.

First and foremost, that every part of my body was bruised and aching. Secondly, that I was lying, facedown, upon the ground. The cold, damp ground.

Lastly, that I wasn't alone. I could hear whispers, couldn't I? And wasn't that something that sounded distinctly like a growl?

You'll think me cowardly, though I'll remind you that I never actually claimed to be all that brave. And even if I had, considering all I'd been through in the last several hours, it might be that my bravery was all used up. Perhaps that is why, for a moment or two, I was tempted to simply lie where I was and not even bother to open my eyes. If I was going to be captured or eaten, what could I do?

You ought to be ashamed of yourself, Mina, I thought. *You didn't get away from the Lord Sarastro only to give up now.*

That was when I heard the voices again, louder this time. I distinctly heard the word *flute.*

That is Lapin's voice! I thought.

I lifted up my head. There was a bear standing right in front of me. The largest I had ever seen, though any bear looks large, I imagine, when you, yourself, are lying flat upon your stomach on the cold, damp ground. It was certainly the angriest bear I had ever seen. Of this there could be no question. Angry with me. There wasn't much doubt about that either.

That was the moment two separate things happened: I discovered just how much I didn't want to be eaten, after all, and the song of the flute began to weave through the air, tantalizing as a whiff of smoke.

How I wish that you could see into my mind! Or

better still, into my heart. For it seemed to me that this was the flute song's intended destination. The bear was just a convenient excuse for the flute to play. My ear, my mind, just convenient conduits for its song to reach my heart. I suppose I could tell you that, with the sound of the flute, the world changed. But the truth, I think, is that it did not.

I was the one who did the changing. For, as the song of the flute wove through me, I realized that I wanted it there, forever. I wanted to make it mine, to not ever let it go.

And this is a very remarkable thing, if you stop to think about it. In fact, as I realized some time later, it's precisely the same as falling in love. For, to do this, your whole being must accept something new, a thing that starts out as foreign, but ends up so much a part of you that your imagination, which is pretty good, fails utterly when trying to imagine life without it.

Still waters run deep, my mother had said, speaking not of my heart, but the heart of some other. But the flute spoke both *to* my heart and *of* it, its song pouring into me straight and true, finding its way to where it belonged as surely as any waterfall finds the pool into which it flows. And no sooner had the flute song reached my heart, than I was changed. For it seemed to me that I was now complete, whereas something had been missing before.

"Mina!" I heard a frantic voice whisper. "Stop daydreaming! Get up!"

And it was only then that I remembered my danger. Remembered Lapin and the great, angry she-bear. I pushed myself upright and saw an astonishing sight. The bear was dancing among the trees, crooning to herself. The song of the flute, or so it seemed, had won her heart also. I couldn't see the one who played it clearly. He—I thought it was a he—moved in and out of the trees, as if trying to draw the bear off.

"Move, Mina," Lapin said again. "You have to get away from the cub."

"What cub?" I asked as I got to my feet and began to move toward him. Lapin was about as far away from the bear as he could get and still be close enough for me to hear him, I couldn't help but notice. At my question, he pointed, and I turned around. Just behind where I had fallen, a bear cub lay curled up, fast asleep. For it, the song of the flute had been as sweet as any lullaby.

"Things should be all right now," Lapin said as he took me by one arm. "You're no longer between the mother and her cub. What are you doing out here, anyhow?"

"I ran away," I said.

"Did you, now?" Lapin asked, and all of a sudden his grin spread wide. "Bet that shook up the Lord Sarastro. Your mother will be proud."

"Oh, Lapin," I said. And I threw my arms around him. I don't think I'd ever been so glad to see someone in my entire life. "How is she? Is she all right?"

"She's just fine," Lapin answered. "It's you we need to be worried about. Come quickly now, Mina. I promised Tern we'd meet him over by those rocks."

"Tern is the one who plays the flute?" I asked as I let Lapin hurry me along.

"That's right."

"Who is he?" I asked.

Lapin shook his head. "That is a question he can best answer for himself. Though he is a prince. I can tell you that much."

"A prince who plays the flute," I said, "rather than use his sword. This fellow may be worth a look."

"You're about to get your chance," Lapin said. "Here he comes."

I turned and saw a young man approaching. His clothing was travel-stained. His hair, the color of warm summer earth. And his eyes . . .

"I think we should be safe now," he said. "Mother and child have been reunited."

I watched as Lapin handed him back his sword.

"Lapin says you are a prince and that your name is Tern," I said.

"Lapin is correct on both counts."

"Tern," I said. "That's a bird's name, isn't it? What did he do, call you with the bells?"

"He did," Tern answered simply. "But he tells me his heart was full of you when he played them."

And at that, the waters of my heart became as

clear as moonlight on a calm lake, and I discovered what it was that the flute had added. What my heart held now that it hadn't before.

"You think you love me," I said, and watched his eyebrows shoot straight up.

"I don't just think it. I know I do," answered Prince Tern, as fearlessly as any dragonslayer ever faced down his adversary. And now he looked me full in the face, his strange eyes meeting the strangeness of mine.

"Will you love me, do you think?" he inquired.

"I might," I replied honestly. "In the meantime, I can tell you this much, though."

"What's that?" he asked.

"I love the color of your eyes."

At this, he smiled. "What color do you see?" he asked.

"One that has no one name," I replied. "For it is comprised of too many things to be called by only one. Your eyes hold all the colors in the world, I think."

"And yours, of the heavens."

"Oh, for pity's sake!" Lapin exclaimed. "Why don't you just give each other a kiss and be done with it? I'm not sure how much longer I can stand this soulful carrying-on. I'll just leave you alone for a while, shall I?"

And so he did.

A thing which, in the end, turned out to be just as well.

Partings

That's right. I did it. I left them alone.

A thing you may wonder at, though, in all honesty, I think the wonder is that I didn't even think twice about it, at the time.

If you could have seen them together. Seen the way they looked into each other's eyes. I imagine that great explorers have this same look, upon finally sighting the new land for which they've spent their whole lives searching. A look of discovery and recognition, all at once. It seemed to me that I could almost hear their hearts change rhythm, striving to find the way to beat as one.

You've heard the saying, *Two's company, three's a crowd?* Of course you have. But I'll bet you didn't know I was the one who coined it. Well, I did. And this was the moment of its inception. The moment Mina and Tern first beheld one another.

It's not as if I went very far, though it may have been farther than I intended. The truth is, I wasn't paying all that much attention to where I was going. I was too busy feeling sorry for myself. A thing I am naturally somewhat embarrassed to admit, but which

I must, for, without this confession, what happened next makes no sense at all.

When will I find love? I thought. Surely, *my* time had come. I was older than the Lady Mina by almost eight years. Not only that, I had been playing the bells, trying to get the music of my heart right, almost literally from the day I was born. Fond as I was of them, one would think, by the law of averages alone, that I would have called to me something other than just another bird by now.

And so I have, I thought. *I called to Tern.*

A thing completely unique in the history of the bells. But, nevertheless, a thing that had ended up being much more important to the Lady Mina's heart than it was to mine.

It was at this point that I stopped my aimless walking and sat down with my back against the nearest tree. Above me loomed a rocky overhang. I took the bells and the hammer from the pack upon my back, settled the bells upon my knee, and cleared my mind. Then, I simply began to play, with no other desire than to hear the sound the bells made, to bring some consolation to my sore and lonesome heart.

I'd like to be able to tell you that the tune I played was sprightly and hopeful. But it was not. Instead, it was the most melancholy set of notes that I had ever brought forth. Filled not with hope, but with fear, and the fear was this: that the future would simply be a continuation of the present. That it would hold no more than the past had held.

You should be ashamed of yourself, Lapin! one part of my mind said. But the other part had a ready answer: *No. Let your melancholy have its voice, for despair is just as true a thing as that which is its opposite.*

And, through the conflict in my own mind, I came to realize a thing I never had before. Always before when I had played the bells, my mind had played an active part. Thinking of the future. Commanding my hands to sound out every hope my mind might conjure. Wondering what the next moment would bring. Would it be another bird, or might this be the song which would, at long last, summon my true love?

But now, abruptly, the battle of my wits had ended in a draw. And so my mind fell silent and withdrew from the fray, leaving behind the thing I should have been listening to all along, of course. To say nothing of playing it.

The music of my heart.

And if, in this moment, both my heart and the music I played were full of despair, what of it? It was the truth, just as true as the love for Mina which had filled my heart when I had played the bells and called to Tern. And so I played of my weariness of summoning birds no matter how beautiful they were, and the pain and pleasure it brought me to be able to call another's true love forth but not my own.

I cannot tell you how long I played. I don't think the heart keeps time the same way the mind does. But, at last, my hands slowed and then grew still, for my heart was still a heart and not a bottomless well. I lifted the hammer above the bells and let it hover there, as if deciding whether or not to play just one more note. And, in that moment, I heard a rustle from the overhanging rock above my head.

I wonder what kind of bird it is this time, I thought.

I looked up. The face of a young woman stared back down.

Dark hair swung over her shoulder in a single plait, so long it seemed to me I might have reached up to tug on the end, though she was high above me. She had eyes as green as the boughs of the tree beneath which I still sat. I felt my heart begin to pound like a fist against a stout oak door.

I don't believe it, I thought.

My playing had called to another human being at last. Surely, she could be no other than my own true love.

Slowly, I got to my feet.

Speak to me, I thought.

And, as if she'd heard me, the young woman's lips parted and she spoke thus:

"Have you lost your mind?"

He stared up at me like the imbecile I was pretty sure he had to be.

"What?"

"It was a simple enough question," I said, trying to keep my voice low. A difficult thing to do when you're calling across even the short distance which separated us.

"Have you lost your mind?" I asked once more. "Don't you know the woods are filled with the Lord Sarastro's soldiers? Do you want them to know where you are?"

"Of course not," he answered automatically. Then I watched as his face paled. "Mercy upon us," he exclaimed, and he spun around. "Mina and Tern."

"You know where Mina is?" I asked. "Where?"

"Not far," he answered as he quickly put away his set of bells. It was the sound of them that had brought me to him in the first place, though I'd been going in the opposite direction at the time. I wasn't quite sure what this meant, but I was quite sure I didn't have the time to think about it now.

"You have to get her out of here," I said.

"I intend to," he said. "Just as soon as you stop talking."

"There's no need to get nasty about it," I said. "Wait a minute and I'll come with you."

I eyed the distance from the edge of the rock to the tree under which he stood, gathered up my skirts, then jumped. I heard his startled exclamation from below as I embraced an armful of pine needles and rough tree bark. Heedless of what it might be doing to the fine garments I still had on, I clambered down.

"What?" I said when I reached the bottom. He was staring at me as if I'd grown a second head. "You never saw a girl climb a tree before?"

"Of course I have," he answered back. "I've just never seen one fly through the air to do it until now. Are you finished playing twenty questions? If so, I suggest we get a move on."

"I'm not the one who was making enough racket to bring the soldiers in the first place, you know," I couldn't help but remark.

"For your information—," he began. But he never finished, for, at that moment, several things happened all at once, and all of them enough to chill the blood.

I heard a man's voice cry out, followed by a quick and vicious clash of arms. A woman's voice, raised sharply in fear. And then, a voice I knew too well.

"Do not harm her, by the Lord Sarastro's command."

Statos, I thought.

"Harm him, and you harm me, too," I heard the Lady Mina say. But I had no time to wonder at the words, for the bell player beside me was starting forward.

"No!" I hissed as I caught him by the arm. I pulled back with all my might and still he dragged me halfway across the tiny clearing where we stood.

"No," I said again, desperate to convince him now.

"Think! Don't just run off. If you go to her aid, they'll catch you, too. Then there will be no one to help her."

At this, he stopped, though I felt the way his body trembled, like a horse longing to lunge out and race.

"How can I help her?" he asked. "Do you know?"

"I do," I said. "At least, I think so. Not far from here, there is a grove that is sacred to the magicians of the Lord Sarastro's order. The lord intended his daughter to be married there this morning. Even if that no longer occurs, it is certainly where he will pass his judgment on her."

"Them," the one beside me corrected automatically. "Don't forget about Tern."

"I can't forget about someone I didn't even know was there," I said.

All of a sudden, his gaze met mine, and I felt that he saw me truly for the very first time.

"You are Gayna," he said. "The daughter of the Lord Sarastro's forrester."

"And what if I am?" I asked. "Now suppose you tell me who you are."

"I am Lapin," he answered simply. "I serve die Königin der Nacht, the Lady Mina's mother. Do you truly wish to aid her?"

"I do," I said. "And we've stood around talking about it long enough. Come on. Let's go."

The Brief Calm Before the Storm

They took Tern's sword, then bound his hands before him, a rope passed between them so that he could be led like an animal. Statos himself tied a thick cloth around Tern's eyes. His hands looked strange, quivering ever so slightly, the veins on the back of them raised, as if there flowed through them some powerful yet suppressed emotion. I realized then how tight was the leash Statos kept upon his self-control. But what he longed to do instead, what it was inside him he was afraid to let burst forth, that thing I could not tell.

When he had finished, he turned back to me. I held out my hands.

"Bind me also. For what you do to Tern, you do to me."

"I will not," he said. "This man is a stranger, but you are the Lord Sarastro's daughter."

"He isn't a stranger," I said. "Not to me."

I saw something that looked like pain come and go in the blue of Statos's eyes.

"Is that why you ran away?" he asked, as if he couldn't help himself. "To meet your sweetheart?"

I gave a sudden laugh. For though that had hardly been my intention when I fled, it was nevertheless a reasonable enough explanation of what had actually occurred.

Color flooded Statos's face. In the next moment, it went bone white.

"You think this is a matter for laughter?" he demanded.

"No," I said. "Of course I don't. But I say again, if you bind him, you must bind me. If not, I'll refuse to budge from this spot and you'll have to carry me like a sack of potatoes. But then you've done that before."

"Mina," Tern said in a low voice.

Statos spun toward him, then. And, in that moment, I saw what it was he held so tight and fast inside. Pain, first. But hard upon its heels was the desire to rid himself of it by inflicting it upon some other. And who better than Tern, who had materialized as if from nowhere and claimed all that Statos had so longed for?

"Let word be sent to the Lord Sarastro that his daughter is found," Statos said after a moment. "Tell him we are on our way to the grove."

The leader of the soldiers saluted smartly. With a flick of his fingers, he gave a signal which sent one of his men scurrying off. Then he turned to Statos.

"Her eyes, at least, must be bound, even if she is the Lord Sarastro's daughter. For the location of the sacred grove is forbidden to all but the members of the lord's order and those who most closely serve them."

"I do not need to be reminded of that," Statos said sharply. Then he pulled in a breath. "Give me a cloth and I will bind her eyes. But, by my command, let her hands remain free."

The soldier gave a second salute. "It shall be as you wish."

And so, for the second time that day, I made a trip in the dark. My eyes wound about with thick, rough cloth. My senses dulled save for the feel of Statos's hands upon mine. How long I walked thus, I cannot tell. But just when I was beginning to feel so weary I couldn't take another step, Statos halted.

"Let the Lady Mina be seated, for she is tired," he said. "But let her eyes remain bound until her father arrives. The other, leave standing. Guard him well."

Other hands moved me gently across what felt like a carpet of soft grass beneath my feet.

"Here is a smooth rock, my lady," a voice said, and I thought I recognized the leader of the soldiers.

"I thank you," I replied. But when his hands fell away, I made no move to sit.

"Will you not take some rest, lady?" he inquired after a moment.

"I will rest when Tern is permitted to," I said, and heard Statos give an exclamation of impatience.

"Leave her to her stubbornness," he called. "We shall see how long it lasts once the Lord Sarastro arrives."

And with that, the clearing filled with silence.

⁂ ⁂ ⁂

"So, what's the plan?" I asked, though I was careful to keep my voice low. "Actually, before we get to that, how do you know where we are going? Surely the location of this grove is supposed to be a secret."

"It is a secret," Gayna said simply. She paused to hold a branch filled with sharply pointed leaves aside so that I might pass by, unscratched, then fell into step beside me. We had been traveling for several minutes, she leading, me following behind, swiftly and in silence. But, at last, my curiosity had gotten the better of me, a thing it has often done.

"None may know where it exists save the members of the lord's order and those who serve them most closely. That is the Lord Sarastro's law," she went on.

"Oh, that's just great," I said. "Now I'm *officially* breaking the lord's law. But you still haven't answered my question. How do you even know where the grove is?"

She turned her head to regard me for a moment, as if trying to weigh how I might take the information she was about to impart.

"I followed the lord and his party one day," she said, her tone matter-of-fact. "Dressed as a boy. No one even noticed I was there, let alone that I wasn't what I seemed to be. Men are often quite unobservant, you know. They see only what they wish to see."

"Particularly those devoted to the sun," I said,

matching my tone to hers as closely as I could. "Their minds lack subtlety, for they look only for what is brightest."

She was silent for a moment. "I hadn't thought of it that way," she finally admitted. "But you could be right. While you, of course, are much less likely to be fooled, as you are accustomed to subtlety, being a servant of the Queen of the Night."

"You catch on fast," I said, and she smiled. "You still haven't answered my first question," I reminded her. "What will we do once we reach the grove?"

"How on earth should I know?"

At this, I stopped and put a hand on her arm to halt her.

"Wait just a minute," I said. "You're saying we're going to rescue Tern and the Lady Mina but we don't know how?"

"I didn't know I was going to help her escape in the first place until I was actually doing it," Gayna said. "So I'm hoping it will be enough just to get to the grove and wait for what comes along."

"That's very brave of you," I said. "Not to mention foolhardy and terrifying."

"All right, let's hear your plan," she said.

"What makes you think I've got one?"

She put her hands on her hips, and a long-forgotten image of my grandmother flashed across my mind.

"In that case, I think you should just shut up about mine," she said.

"What do you mean yours?" I asked. "You haven't got one either!"

"For heaven's sake," she hissed. "Keep your voice down. What, precisely, would you like to do? Something, or nothing?"

"Something, of course," I said. "I'd just like to know what it is ahead of time."

"We do know what it is," she said. "We're going to help the Lady Mina and what's-his-name."

"Tern."

"Tern. The fact that we don't have all the details worked out yet doesn't mean we won't be successful. Now can we please stop talking and keep on going? Preferably in silence, which I understand is golden. I never in my entire life met anyone so devoted to making noise as you."

"And I never met anyone so argumentative," I said. But by then I was talking to her back. So I did the only thing I could.

I followed.

I saw the Lord Sarastro for the very first time standing with the sun behind him. A thing I'm absolutely certain he did on purpose, for he was absolutely blinding. And, for a moment, I must admit, my heart quailed. For it seemed to me there was no difference between the lord and the sun itself.

How can I set my will against such a one and survive, I wondered, *let alone, triumph?* Then, in the next moment, I answered my own fear with hope. *Because I will do more than stake my will. I will stake my heart, also.*

But it would not be alone. Mina's would be with it. My eyes did not have far to look for her. Her father had placed her at his side, her eyes now unbound, and in them an expression that reminded me to hope.

And when I saw this, the brilliance of the Lord Sarastro seemed to dim, and I noticed that, though the light was bright, it was also low in the sky. The hours of the day were growing short. Soon, the night would come.

But if the Lord Sarastro were in a hurry because of this, he did not show it.

"I am told you are called Tern," he said. "And that you are a prince in your own country. Are these things true?"

I bowed my head. "They are, my lord."

At this, the lord motioned to the soldier who stood beside me. "Let his hands be unbound," he commanded. "For if I take his word about these things, then I must trust that he is a man of honor."

And so, at last, I stood unbound before Mina's father and all whom he had gathered to him in this place that was most sacred to the magicians of his order.

"Why have you come here?" he inquired.

"Surely the Lord Sarastro must know that

already," I answered. "For I was brought here by his followers."

At this, the lord's lips twitched, whether in irritation or amusement, I could not tell.

"A clever answer," he commented. "Let us hope, for your sake, you are clever with more than just your tongue. Why have you come into my country, Prince Tern? That is the thing that I would know. Speak true, for I will know if you are lying."

"I followed where my heart led, my lord."

"And it led you to my daughter, is that what you're trying to tell me?"

"It did," I replied.

"And what would your heart ask of me?"

"That you give your blessing to Mina becoming my wife. For, this, we both desire."

"Do you, indeed?" said the Lord Sarastro. "What do you have to say to this, Mina?" he asked, turning to her abruptly. "You have kept silent long enough."

"The Lord Sarastro has not addressed me until this moment," Mina said. "But since he has now, I will say this: Prince Tern speaks the truth, as you commanded. Therefore, I have nothing to add."

"You desire to be his wife."

"I do, my lord."

"And what of the prophecy spoken at the hour of your birth? What of the pains I have taken to choose a husband for you? Do these things mean nothing?"

"What should they mean to me?" Mina inquired.

"You have dedicated yourself to the prophecy, not to me. You do not know me, Father. Why should your mind choose for me, while my own heart goes ignored?"

"Father," the Lord Sarastro said, and, to my surprise, I heard bitterness in his tone. "You call me that now, only when you want something from me."

"Which only goes to prove I am your true daughter," Mina responded. "For you have not claimed me until now, to help you fulfill your own desire."

"And you think you know what that is," the Lord Sarastro said. A statement, a challenge.

"But surely it is obvious," Mina replied. "To marry me to the one of your choice, and so control the outcome of the prophecy. On the day I wed, the world will change. That cannot be altered. But you would try to have the world change according to your will. That is why you broke your own oath, and stole me away before the proper time.

"You do not think of me, but only of protecting your own power. If your efforts to this end mean nothing to me, we are even, I think. For my happiness means nothing to you."

"Of course it does," the Lord Sarastro protested, shocked.

"Then prove it. Let me marry Tern."

"My lord!" the one called Statos suddenly burst out, as if he could hold himself in check no longer. "You cannot give your consent to such a thing. He is a stranger, unproven and unknown."

"Then let me make a trial and prove myself," I said at once, and I stepped forward, a thing which made the Lord Sarastro's soldiers lay hands upon their swords. "For then I will be a stranger no longer. My worth shall be known."

"You would undergo any trial I set?" the Lord Sarastro asked, and I could not read the expression in his eyes.

"I would, my lord," I answered steadily. And I held those eyes I could not understand with my own.

"Without fear?" the lord asked softly.

"Of course not," I replied. "But fear is no fit means to measure anyone, for fools have no fear, or so I've heard it said."

"And so have I," the Lord Sarastro said, and he released my eyes. "That is well spoken. Very well. Let you and Statos face the same trials together. By the outcome Mina's husband will be chosen."

I heard Mina draw in a quick breath, but before she could object, Statos spoke once more.

"How can you propose to test me like some stranger?" he demanded, and all there assembled must have heard the pain in his voice. "I have been your apprentice, and your choice to wed the Lady Mina, for many years. I have no need to prove myself."

"Perhaps not," the Lord Sarastro said. "But my mind speaks that this is the only way to be fair to all. Therefore, it is my will that you undergo these trials."

"I tell you, I will not!" Statos shouted. "For you do not use your mind in this, but your heart. And not even yours, I think, but your daughter's. You do the very thing you have sworn you would not. Already you have broken one oath. Now it seems you will break another."

The Lord Sarastro's face flushed bright red.

"Enough!" he roared. "Either face the trials that I will set or give up all claim to Mina's hand."

"My lord," Statos said, his voice strangled as if holding himself in check only by the force of his will. "I will not, nor is that all. For I call upon those members of our order here assembled to witness the fact that you do me a great wrong.

"But I will stay while this prince faces his trials, and see the outcome. For he may fail, and, in his failure I may see my triumph."

"As you will," the Lord Sarastro said, and now I heard nothing but weariness in his voice. He turned to me. "Prince Tern," he said. "Hear now the nature of your trials. Carrying what you have with you in this moment but no more, you must pass through the fires of hell unscathed and return from the embrace of Death alive.

"If you can do these things, my daughter will be yours."

There was one moment of absolute silence. Then Statos laughed, and the sound was like the clash of sword on shield, metallic and harsh.

"But surely these are impossible tasks," he said.

"How fortunate for you, then, that you refused them," I heard the Lady Mina answer softly.

Statos flushed and took a step toward her. But, at a signal from the Lord Sarastro, the members of their order held Statos back.

"Do you accept these trials, Prince Tern?" the lord asked.

"I do accept them," Tern answered in a steady voice.

And then, to the astonishment of all present, with the possible exception of me, for I knew her well, the Lady Mina stepped forward. In fact, so great was their astonishment that it seized all their limbs and held them fast. They made no move to stop her. And so, she walked across the circle and took Tern by the hand, gazing for a moment into his eyes.

"You are certain?" he asked.

"Absolutely," she said. Only then did she turn to face her father. "I accept them also."

"It is well that you do," the Lord Sarastro said. "For you may not balk at the outcome. Now let him go, that the trials may commence."

He still doesn't understand, I thought. *But, then, how can he? For he doesn't really know her.*

"I don't think you understand, Father," Mina said. "I will not stay behind like a small child to await an outcome decided by others. Tern is the one my heart has chosen. Where he goes, even into danger, I will go, also, for that is where I belong."

"Do not be so foolish, Mina!" the lord exclaimed, and I realized then that this possibility had simply never entered his mind. "The trials are for Tern, to determine his worthiness."

"And what of my own worthiness?" Mina inquired. "Or is that already decided for no other reason than that I am your daughter? You treat me like a prize at the village carnival, my Lord Sarastro. But I am not some thing for you to give away. I am myself. I have a mind and heart of my own. And both say this: I will go with Tern. I will not stay behind."

Slowly the Lord Sarastro moved to where his daughter stood, took her face gently between his hands, and tipped it up.

"It seems you have been telling the truth," he said at last. "For I think I do not know you at all. But this much I can see for myself: that your mind is set. Very well. You may go with Prince Tern."

"No! Wait!" I cried.

For, in that moment, I saw that it was not only Mina who had spoken true. Gayna had spoken the truth, also. A time to aid Mina and Tern had, indeed, presented itself. Not in the way we might have hoped, for escape was plainly impossible. But, if there's one thing life has taught me, it's to be prepared for anything.

And so, I dropped down from the tree in which I had been hiding, much to the delight of Mina and Tern and the consternation of the Lord Sarastro and his soldiers.

"Lapin!" Mina cried.

"Spy!" the Lord Sarastro said, and he signaled his soldiers forward. "How did you come to know about this place? How long have you been here?"

"Which question would you have me answer first?" I managed to get out before the soldiers surrounded me and pinned me fast by both arms.

"I'd show a little more respect, if I were you," the Lord Sarastro said.

I did my best to make a bow. Difficult, given my present circumstances. "You misunderstand my intentions, my lord. I wish only to give your daughter a gift."

"What gift?"

"If I might have the use of my arms?"

At a nod from the lord, the soldiers released me, though they stood close and tense as I reached inside my cloak.

"The bells!" Mina exclaimed when she saw what I intended to give. "Oh, Lapin."

"Bells," the Lord Sarastro said. "You wish to give my daughter a set of bells?"

"It is all I have to give," I said simply. "For she has had my heart from a week after she was born. She may not carry a weapon, is this not so? But surely she may take a gift from an old friend. It is only a simple set of bells."

"There is nothing simple about these bells, I think," the Lord Sarastro said, and he came close to study them, though he made no move to take them from me. "For I have heard tales of them before now."

"Do not permit this, lord," Statos burst out suddenly. "You cannot trust him. He serves the Queen of the Night."

"That is so," I answered. "But I am also myself. I have my own will. I know my mind, my heart. That is more than you can say, I think."

"Enough!" commanded the Lord Sarastro. "I will permit this gift if you answer me this question: How did you come to know the location of this grove?"

"I told him," Gayna said. And she dropped down beside me, her skirts flaring like a great golden bell.

"Gayna," Lord Sarastro said. "I suppose I should have known."

"The hour grows late, my lord." Statos spoke up once more. "The sun is going down. You should make a decision, and let the trials commence."

"Give my daughter your gift, Lapin," the Lord Sarastro said. "Then let Tern and Mina be taken to the place of trial."

Trial the First, and Trial the Second

Any person of sense would have been absolutely terrified.

But, as I think my story's already proved, the one with sense in my family is my younger brother, Arthur. He's the one who took the traditional route, inheriting a kingdom from our father. Me, I set out to roam the wide world to see if I could find my heart. And I had done so.

Naturally, having been successful, I wanted to live as long and happy a life as I possibly could. I'm not a complete idiot, after all. As Mina and I followed the Lord Sarastro to the place where we would undergo our trials, my heart did beat quickly, it is true, but more with anticipation than with fear. My heart had accomplished its mission. It had found its match. No trial Mina's father or anyone else might set could take that away from me.

Not far from the location of the sacred grove, the trees of the forest gave way altogether, and the sheer rock of the mountain itself rose straight up in a great wall. Upon its face were carved a series of symbols, all depicting the sun on its path across the sky. The Lord

Sarastro moved to the one in the very center, where the sun was at its fullest and brightest, and struck the image three times with the staff of his order.

At that, with a motion that was all the more astonishing for the fact that it was accomplished in perfect silence, a door in the rock wall swung open. A series of white stone steps plunged straight down. As I stared at them, I felt a sudden burst of fierce heat.

The fires of hell, I thought.

"This is your last chance to turn back," the Lord Sarastro said. "Once you have set your feet upon this path, there is no other course but down. If you walk the path to the very end, you will be successful and emerge upon the other side. If not, you will be lost forever in the bowels of the very earth itself. No power in the universe will be able to call you back.

"Do you still accept these trials?"

"I do, my lord," I answered steadily, and felt the way Mina's hand tightened upon mine.

"And I do, also," she vowed.

"Then let these trials commence," the Lord Sarastro said. "And may the strength of that which you hold in your hearts be your shield and your reward."

"I can't believe I'm thinking this," Mina said as we made our way down. We had been moving steadily downward for the space of no more than a few minutes. Already, the heat was near to overwhelming.

And now we could hear the fire's roar. It had a voice like a living thing, a hungry predator whose only thought is to devour.

"What?" I asked.

"We're facing trials which could end our lives," Mina went on. "But all I can think is, who knew that hell was so close? Just a short flight of stairs away."

"Perhaps it is some magic of your father's," I suggested.

"Perhaps," Mina agreed. "And perhaps hell is this close to us every single day. Perhaps it is only our commitment to joy which holds it down, for do not those who give up joy claim to suffer hell on earth?"

"I have heard it said so," I acknowledged, and gripped her hand all the tighter. I could feel the way the sweat pooled in the very center of her palm, but whether from the heat or from fear I could not tell.

"It's getting hotter, Tern," Mina gasped. "Do you hear the way the fire roars? The path and walls have a strange glow. Do you see it?"

I nodded, for I did see it. The white stone on which we walked was stained red as blood.

"I think we are very close now. Are you sorry you came with me?"

"Of course not," Mina said. "Now is hardly the time to start asking silly questions. You should save your strength."

"Just one thing first," I said.

And I took her in my arms and kissed her. The

first kiss that we had shared. It wasn't much like other first kisses, I think. Her lips weren't smooth as rose petals, but dry and chapped from the heat of the fires of hell. But the touch of them so filled my heart with music that, for the instants the kiss lasted, I no longer heard the fire nor felt its heat. All I heard was the music of my own heart. All I felt was joy.

When it was over, Mina lifted a hand to my cheek.

"Your eyes are as white as ice," she said.

I smiled. "Let us hope it is ice enough to put this fire out." Then, still hand in hand, we turned to face the fire's glow. As it turned out, Mina was right.

Hell was close.

The turn of the very next corner brought an end to the passage. Here, in spite of all my joy, all my desire to be brave, I stopped short. Before us, a great lake of rippling flame spread out. So vast, it completely filled my vision, even when I turned my head from side to side. It had no end, this lake of flame.

This is the worst thing about hell, I thought. Not the heat, and not the pain, though these were horrible enough. But most horrible of all was that it had no end. Once hell takes you, you are there forever. There is no way out.

"How do we cross? Can you see?" I asked.

For, as I stood there, it seemed to me that my eyes began to dim, and the only sense I truly possessed was that of my ears, and they were filled with the fire's roar. Then I felt Mina's touch upon my arm.

"There, Tern. I see a way!" she said.

I shook my head to clear my vision, and looked to where she pointed.

Across the lake of fire, like an arm reaching out to ask for help, stretched a single span of stone. From where I stood, I judged it wide enough for two people to walk side by side, but not a single step wider. Hungry tongues of fire lapped up at its deck. With every step we took, Mina and I would feel their touch. Yet the Lord Sarastro had said we must pass through the fires of hell unscathed, unharmed. If we could not, we would lose the trial. Then Death himself would come to claim us.

You are a fool, Tern, I thought. *What makes you think you are strong enough or clever enough to brush back the fires of hell? You couldn't even succeed your own father, claim your own birthright. You will fail, for you are nothing.*

And no sooner had I thought these things than it seemed to me that I understood the fire's roar. It was not one single voice, as I had previously perceived, but a multitude of voices, all raised at one and the self-same time. Each crying out its own doom. But more than that, mine.

"This one thinks the Lord Sarastro will abandon his daughter in this place!" I heard one call out. And it seemed to me every single voice the fire held laughed in response.

"If so, he is an idiot and deserves his fate," a

second observed. "For surely the lord will rescue his daughter at the last moment."

"Rescue her, leave this one here, then marry his daughter to the man of his own choice," put in a third voice. "That's what a smart father would do, and the Lord Sarastro is no fool."

I am lost, I thought.

It seemed to me that the voices of the fires of hell made perfect sense. Why should the Lord Sarastro abandon the daughter he so loved to a horrible fate when he might save her? His claim that no power on earth could save us was surely a lie. A lie to trick me into putting myself in harm's way so that he could be rid of me and bestow Mina where he pleased: on Statos.

Darkness filled all my vision, my knees gave way, and I sank down. At once, the call of the fire increased. So many voices that I could not distinguish between them anymore. But I knew what they said. In my heart, I knew it, for did they not speak what my heart feared most?

There was no point in trying, for I would fail. No point in hoping, for I was already lost.

How long I stayed so, I cannot tell you, for it is a thing I do not know. I'm not even sure time is measured in the regular way in that terrible place. But, slowly, gradually, I began to hear a new sound. A sound that was not a voice of the fire, but a voice from the world above. Mina's voice.

"Tern! Tern!" I heard her cry, and her voice was dry and hoarse. As if she had been calling my name over and over, for a very long time. And in her voice I heard fear. I heard sorrow and pain.

You might think that hearing such things in Mina's voice would have increased the fear and pain in my own heart. But they did not. Instead, at the sound of her voice, my heart opened, just a crack. Fear receded. Love and hope returned. And in that moment, I perceived that I had misjudged hell. It was stronger and more terrible than even I had imagined, for I had thought it was a place that was simply external. I knew now that it was not, for the seeds of hell are sown in each and every heart.

Hell is pain. An agony which goes on forever. And you choose it for yourself.

I will not! I thought.

"Mina," I gasped out. With one hand, I scrabbled at the front of my tunic. "Mina, help me. . . ."

"See how pitiful he is," the voices of hell jeered at me. "He refuses to admit what must come, even now."

With a cry of frustration, I tore the fabric of my tunic, exposing the place where the flute lay in its sheath, just above my heart.

"Mina," I said again, and felt her hands upon mine, willing them to be still.

"It's all right, Tern. I understand what you would have me do," she said. "But, in spite of your pain, I think the solution to this trial is for my heart to solve, not yours. For I have watched your suffering, and longed to end it, and is that not what love does? But only if you trust me."

"I will. I do," I said. And I watched her smile. Her face was red and splotched with tears. Her hair was in wild disarray, as if she had pulled it in frustration. Never had I seen a more beautiful sight.

"Then let us see if I am right," she said. "And whether I am or not, remember this: I love you, Tern."

"And I you," I said.

At this, with some effort, Mina helped me to my feet. And, as she did so, the fires of hell fell silent, as if they could do no more. Whether this was a good sign or a bad one, I could not yet tell. Not that it mattered, anymore.

I had made my choice. I would trust in Mina. If we failed, we would do so together, not because I had chosen my own despair, chosen hell over the woman I loved.

Mina pushed back her cloak and pulled out Lapin's bells, glowing red and gold. She cradled them in the crook of one arm, as one does an infant.

"Walk by my side, for that is your place," my true love said.

Then she turned her face to the fire and set her foot upon the stone bridge, and, at the exact same moment, she began to play the bells.

This is the song that the Lady Mina played: the

story of our love. She played its unexpectedness, the long odds of its ever existing in the first place. She played its sweetness and its joy. She played its determination and its strength. But she played of its uncertainties, also. For not even the strongest love is proof against all fears. Had I not just proved that, myself?

And no sooner had she played of love's uncertainties than her song passed beyond any description that I can give you, for what she played was no longer just a song of love. It had become the thing itself.

Below us, alongside us, in perfect silence now, the flames of hell writhed. They reached for us with every step we took, fingers of flame curling greedily upward, held back only by the sound of Mina's bells. Then, high above us, a new sound began to fill my ears. The beat of wings. I lifted my face up, and saw that all the air above us was filled with fluttering white.

Doves, I thought.

And, suddenly, I understood what it was that Mina had done. In playing love itself, she had played much more than the love for me which filled her heart. She played all the love that she had ever known, or hoped to know. Her love for her mother. Her love for Lapin. And the birds which so loved him had answered the call of the bells.

In a great flurry of white wings, they swooped down around us. And, at the beating of their wings, the very fires of hell fell back and were put out. A fine layer of ash rose into the air, so that my nose and mouth were clogged, and my eyes watered. But it clung most tenaciously to the doves.

Now, at last, they opened their throats as well as their wings, and, at the sound of their calls, Mina stilled the voice of the bells. Together, we listened to the doves' lament for their fine, white wings. And for this reason, forever after, have they borne the name *mourning doves.*

Still making their soft, sad calls, they rose into the air in a great, gray spiral. Up, up, up they flew, one after the other, and then were gone. I don't know where they went to any more than I know where they had come from. But I think now as I did then, that they were summoned by the power of love.

And with their going, the first trial was over. Mina and I had crossed the bridge, unscathed by the fires of hell.

"One down, one to go," Mina said. And through the ashes that stained her face, she smiled.

At the far side of the bridge over the flames of hell was a great cavern. In spite of its size, it had been hidden from us until now. For the fires of hell burned so hot, so bright and high, that they had obscured anything that might have lain beyond them.

"Do you suppose this is what the underworld truly is?" Tern asked quietly as we stood side by side. "A series of never-ending rooms, one after the other? A great labyrinth of trials?"

"I do not know," I said. "I know only that we must go inside. We cannot come to the end if we do not move forward."

But even as I spoke, I felt dismay seize my heart. For the cavern before us was as bright as day, hewn from the same white stone as the path which, all along, Tern and I had followed. And it was cold as ice. Across its great distance, I could discern a small, black opening at the far end. Along its walls stretched two great wings of darkness, one to the right and one to the left. And it was these which made my heart, so lately brave, go still with fear.

"Look, Tern," I cried. "Surely those must be the wings of Death, himself. Perhaps he is a great, black bird. A carrion crow. I cannot play the bells in this place. For if I do, I will not beat back Death. Instead, I will summon him."

And at this, I began to weep, for it seemed to me that I had offered only false hope. I had brought us this far only to fail, and our lives and love would be utterly extinguished by Death's embrace. I could not win this trial.

"I think you must be right," Tern said after a moment. "For crows are clever, and surely this is the most clever trap of all. See how the reach of the wings is almost upon us? All we need do is take a step and Death's arms will be around us. The trial will be over as soon as it begins."

"I don't know what to do," I said.

"Mina," Tern said. "Let me see your eyes. But dry them first. I cannot see truly if you weep."

And so I did as he asked. I ceased to weep and looked into his eyes.

"Tell me what you see," he said.

"Myself," I answered. "And that is all. Your eyes have no color in this place."

"And when I look into your eyes," Tern answered, "I see myself, and that is all. Perhaps that is the answer to this riddle. In this place, we have only one another. You aided me in my fear; now I will aid you in yours."

"But how?"

"I will deal honorably with Death," Tern said. "I will not try to cheat him or outsmart him, for he is ready for such things. He has laid his trap too well."

So saying, he reached inside his torn tunic and pulled out the flute that he had carved.

"The first time I played this," Tern continued, "my father said he thought the beauty of its music would make even Death pause in his course. I will give Death an offering no one else has thought to give. I will give him beauty. Let us see if he may be charmed. But only if you trust me in this. If it is your wish, as well as mine."

"It is," I said, and found that hope had returned to my heart once more.

"Then stay by my side," Tern said, his words once again echoing my own. "For that is where you belong."

"I will," I said. "And let us not be parted, whatever comes."

"That is my wish also," Tern said.

And now, at last, he raised the flute to his lips and pulled a deep breath into his lungs. The fires of hell no longer burned. The ashes their passing had left behind had all been carried away by the mourning doves. And so, in that moment, my true love pulled in a pure, true breath. And, in the next, he breathed out, and I heard the flute's song.

High and sweet was the sound it made, as high and sweet as the hopes for the future which Tern and I both held in our hearts. A future that acknowledged Death would come at the end.

Oh, Tern, I thought.

For it seemed to me, as I listened, that I understood the meaning of his song. I had played of love, of life. But Tern played of the end of these things, or at least the end as living beings may know them. His was a song that did not deny Death, but gave him his due, as all things which live and breathe must.

Accept this gift, I thought, *as we will accept your embrace, one day. But for now, let us pass. For our day is not yet come.*

The great wings of darkness began to quiver, and, for a moment, I could have sworn I felt my heart stop. Then, the great wings of Death fell back. The bands of darkness vanished from the cavern walls. In the opening at the far end of the cavern, a small figure stood alone.

I touched Tern's arm. Still playing, he nodded his head to show he understood. To move forward was no longer to enter Death's embrace. And so, the flute still at his lips, Tern and I walked across the cavern which separated life from death, in the same way we had crossed the fires of hell, side by side. Until, at last, we stood before Death himself.

He wasn't a bird after all, but a small, wizened man, his body wrapped in a threadbare cloak. Still, Tern played his music. And so, I seized my courage with both hands, pulled in my own deep breath, and looked into Death's fathomless eyes.

I am not presumptuous enough to say that I understood or even recognized everything I saw there. But, where it seemed to me that Tern's eyes held all the possibilities in the world, at least for me, the eyes of Death held all the possibilities for everyone. For, sooner or later, all possibilities come down to just one thing: the moment Death finally takes us in his arms.

With my own eyes, I asked a question. And it was then that the last thing I expected happened. Death smiled. Showing a set of perfectly straight and even white teeth in that crooked old face. Then, like a rusty door hinge, he pivoted slowly on one heel and stepped aside. Together, Tern still playing the flute, the two of us moved past him and through the far door of that great cavern.

And so the second of our trials was done.

In Which Many Stories Draw Down to a Single Close

They stepped back into the open air just as the sun went down. Tern, with the flute still at his lips. Mina, with the bells that I had given her cradled in the crook of one arm.

At the sight of them, a great shout went up among the Lord Sarastro's followers. Statos fell to his knees, his head bowed down. The lord himself rushed forward. As I saw the look upon his face, I realized that his heart had not truly believed he would see his daughter again until that moment.

As for me, I'd had no doubts. But then I'd known Mina much longer than the Lord Sarastro had, even if he was her father.

"Mina," he said, and his voice was filled with many things, but chief among them joy and wonder. "My child. My daughter."

"Sarastro, Mage of the Day," she answered. "Father."

Now, finally, Tern lowered the flute, and its song fell silent.

"Prince Tern," the Lord Sarastro said. "If you will let me, I will embrace you as my son."

"With all my heart," Tern said. And so it was done.

"At the first light of day tomorrow, you will wed," the Lord Sarastro went on.

Still trying to control everything, I thought.

"Say by the light of the full moon instead," Tern suggested quietly. "For I will not marry Mina without the presence of her mother."

"Well spoken, Prince Tern!" a voice I recognized all too well said.

There followed several moments of confusion while the servants of the Mage of the Day and those of the Queen of the Night got used to the presence of one another, a thing that had not happened in years beyond count. In the midst of this, Statos suddenly rose to his feet and rushed forward. He threw himself at my mistress's feet.

"Hear me, great queen!" he cried.

At this, complete silence fell over all assembled.

"I will hear any who makes a just petition," my mistress answered quietly. "Stand, that I may see your face, and identify yourself."

"I am called Statos," he said as he got to his feet. "Chosen apprentice of the Lord Sarastro until this moment. But, as he broke his oath to you and stole your daughter before the appointed time, so did he break his word to me when he said that she might be my bride. But, if you will give me what I ask, I will render up all my lord's secrets to you, and you will have great power over him.

"So will the world be changed indeed when the

Lady Mina weds, and all in your favor, if you will consent that she shall be my wife."

"Let me see if I understand you," my mistress said. "You would wed my daughter though you know she has given her heart to another."

"Lady, I would," answered Statos.

The Queen of the Night was silent for many moments. "But why?" she asked at last. "What joy could there be in such a life for you?"

"Perhaps I do not look for joy," Statos said, "but only for the honoring of a promise. I have been taught that such things have much value."

"And so they do," replied die Königin der Nacht. "Yet, for all that, you plead with the wrong person. No one may honor the promise of another, just as no one may give another's heart.

"If you ask me, I will share your grief at the promise broken. But I will not replace it with one that I must break, myself. My daughter is not for you. Let her go, Statos."

"I cannot," he said softly.

"May I speak?" Tern suddenly asked.

"To me, most certainly," my mistress answered. She regarded Statos thoughtfully for a moment. "I suggest you listen to what Prince Tern has to say. He has just proved his worthiness in a rather spectacular fashion, after all."

So Statos turned, and the two men faced one another.

"Will you gloat, then?" Statos asked.

"Of course not," Tern said, his voice showing

clearly that such a thought had never occurred to him, and, at the sound of it, Statos blushed.

"I would offer you a gift, if you will take it."

Statos's eyelids flickered, as if sheer force of will alone kept him from looking in Mina's direction.

"There is only one thing you possess which I want."

"By which you mean Mina, I suppose." Tern sighed. "Remarks like that only show how much you're the wrong man for her, Statos. I don't possess her at all. But I'm not trying to argue. I'm trying to offer you this."

He held out the flute.

"I carved this on the night that Mina was abducted," he explained. "Though I did not know that at the time. It is carved from the heart of the most ancient and powerful oak tree in all my father's country. The King's Oak, it is called. And as my hands shaped it, this was my desire: to create that which would let me know my own heart."

He turned then, and smiled at Mina.

"This, I have done. But when I look at you, Statos, I see one who has not yet discovered what his heart holds. So I would give the flute to you, in the hope that you might use it to find your own happiness. My need for it is over."

"You think I want your charity?" Statos asked, his voice strangled. "Your used possessions?"

"I'm trying to give you a gift," Tern said. "The greatest I have to bestow. Will you not take it? Will you not be my friend, and Mina's, rather than our enemy?"

Statos took a breath. But before he could speak, Gayna broke in.

"Take it," she said. "Take it, Statos." And it was she, rather than Mina, who stepped to Tern's side. "All your life you have lived by the rules of another. Worked so that his dreams, his desires, might be given life, even the desire to make the Lady Mina your wife.

"You told me once that you had always been free to choose. Now you stand in the place to which all your choices have brought you. You are betrayed and alone. Why should you reject such a rich gift? Take it, and learn what your own heart holds."

"You would have me take this gift, then," Statos said.

"I would," Gayna answered.

"And if it tells me that I should leave?"

"Then go. Look forward, not back."

"Would you wait for me?" asked Statos.

This was the moment I discovered I was holding my breath, had been holding it, in fact, from the time that Gayna first stepped forward.

"No, I would not," Gayna answered softly. "For I, too, am done with living my life according to the desires of one who does not love me. Instead, I will stay, and see if my heart holds what I think it might."

And with that, she looked straight at me, and I felt my heart roll over once.

"You would have me be alone, then?" Statos asked.

"Well, of course I would," Gayna answered, as if she thought he was downright silly. "But only for the time it takes to know yourself. How long a time that ends up being is up to you, I think."

At this, Statos looked Tern full in the face, and, for the first time, it was with no anger coloring his own.

"I will accept your gift with thanks," he said, "and wish you and the Lady Mina much joy together."

And so, Tern handed him the flute and Statos accepted it. Then he bowed, and turned as if to go. At that moment, I heard a rush and sweep of wings. *That is the nightingale,* I thought. But, instead of settling upon my shoulder, she settled upon Statos's. She ruffled her feathers once, twice, as if accustoming herself to this new perch, then opened her beak, and poured forth her song.

Never had I heard her sing a song so beautiful. But the most astonishing thing was yet to come. For, no sooner had she finished, than Statos put the flute to his lips and let the notes fly forth. And the song he played was so lovely, yet so sad, that all eyes were filled with tears when he had done.

Then the nightingale flew from his shoulder, singing as she went, and, as if spellbound, Statos followed, wrapping his own song around the nightingale's notes. They may be traveling together still, for all I know. For with his departure, he leaves this story forever, and where he is now or what became of him, I do not know.

Though I hope he's happy, don't you?

Finale

Come close, and I will finish a story, for the end is very near, now. Tern and I were married that very night, by the light of the full moon, while my father's retainers and my mother's danced together on the ground, and the stars turned reels in the overhanging sky.

The revels ended just at dawn. For then, as they had for untold years, my parents prepared to part company. But, before this could happen, I had my own gift to give. One I had discussed beforehand with Lapin, for it required his blessing.

"You are sure?" I asked.

"I am," he replied, and he had Gayna at his side. "We may not be quite as sudden in our love as you and Tern are, but then we are small folk, not great ones."

"Speak for yourself," Gayna said.

At which Lapin laughed. "Have I ever mentioned that my middle name is Robert?"

"Why should you wish to be called anything other than what you are?" Gayna inquired.

"That's it," Lapin said. "Now I'm sure it's love."

And so, as the musicians at last fell silent, and the tired dancers sat upon the ground, I went to stand in the center of my father's sacred grove and called my parents to stand by my side.

"Mother, Queen of the Night," I said, "and Mage of the Day, my father, I have a gift for you, if you will accept it. But only if you both agree, for it must belong to both of you, or to neither."

"She sounds just like you," my mother observed.

"She does not," my father protested. "I'm nowhere near that pompous and stuffy."

"You think not?" my mother asked, and I could see the way her eyes danced with laughter in the thinning dark.

"Do you suppose I might speak for just a moment?" I inquired. "I'd like to get this done before the sun comes up. The timing of this is sort of important."

"I apologize, Mina," my mother said. "Please, go on. And of course I accept your gift, even if it means I must share it with your father."

"Anything your mother can do, I can do," declared the Lord Sarastro.

I sincerely hope this works, I thought. And I held out Lapin's bells.

"You know the history of these bells," I said. "But I think they have a future, also. In order for it to be fulfilled, you each must answer the same question: Do you love each other?"

Not a soul stirred in the clearing as we waited for my parents to answer. "Speak from your hearts," I charged. "Anything less doesn't count, and not only that, it will bring about disaster."

"Then from my heart, I answer this," said the Lord Sarastro. "That though I do not always understand her, I do truly love your mother."

"And I say this," my mother replied. "That I love your father, though he has wronged me. And because I love truly, I forgive those wrongs."

"Then these belong to you," I said. "To both of you, equally, to share and share alike. To the Lord Sarastro in the day, and to Pamina, die Königin der Nacht, in the dark.

"Each day as the sun sets, Father, you must give them to my mother. And each day as the sun rises, Mother, you must give them to my father. Let the rising and setting of the sun be a time of coming together, not of dividing. Play the bells, and let all creation hear the music of your hearts, for you have hidden it away for far too long."

"Actually, I think you're right. She does sound like me," my father said.

My mother laughed and took the bells from my arms. She had time to sound just one note, but it was a note of such incredible beauty and joy that it caused the sun to leap straight up over the horizon. Then my mother turned and gave the bells to my father.

"I will be interested to hear the song you play," she said.

And now my father laughed in his turn. "And so will I."

Then he began to play, and at this, the full glory of the world burst forth. For, in that moment, the hopes of the powers that watch over the universe were fulfilled, and the world was discovered to be much more than a mountain, albeit a very tall one, but an entire globe, spinning in the sky.

And with this discovery, day and night no longer warred with one another. For, in its new shape, the world could never be all one thing or all the other. The night that I was married is the time night and day began to live side by side in the world, a circumstance with which you are familiar, for it has existed ever since that time.

In time, the music my parents play came to be known as the music of the spheres. It may still be called this, for all I know. For they are still playing. They will play until the last gasp of the universe itself. You can hear them for yourself, if your heart knows how to listen.

And as for me and Tern, we did not settle in just one place, but decided to spend our days wandering through the new world which had just been born. Naturally we stop to see both his family and mine upon our travels, at holiday and birthday time, as often as can be managed.

But I think the truth is that neither Tern nor I needs a fixed place, as other people do, for the true place of each is in the heart of the other. That will be true for as long as our hearts beat and maybe even longer. I don't yet know.

So here, I think, is where the story ends. Or at least the portion of it I am able to tell you.

Author's notes

This story was inspired by my favorite opera: Mozart's *Die Zauberflöte. The Magic Flute.* That's right. I said opera. Not only that, I said I liked it. Why do you think they put author notes at the end of the book and not the beginning, if not to avoid scaring readers off entirely?

Seriously, though. You ought to try it. Opera is so fantastical, so much bigger than life. It's not all overweight sopranos marching around in weird costumes that always seem to involve helmets with great curved horns sticking out of the top. And *Die Zauberflöte* is a great place to start.

There's even a film version by the great Swedish filmmaker Ingmar Bergman, which is one of my favorite movies on the entire planet. In fact, it was Bergman, not Mozart, who first created a husband and wife relationship for Sarastro and the Queen of the Night. It seems just right, though. What has always appealed to me about this story is its combination of whimsy and distress. Of sunlight and shadow. Yes, this would explain my title. I'm also drawn to the notion that, to truly win what your heart desires, you must conquer your own fears. In our own ways, we all face trials.

I've definitely reshaped some elements to fit my world view, rather than Mozart's. The truth is, men didn't think much of women, or at least not of their brains, in Mozart's time. In the original trials, Tern (named Tamino in the opera) is steadfast and brave, and Pamina mostly tags along. And the character of Statos (Monostatos, in the opera) is strictly a bad guy for no other reason than that he's a Moor. So there's definitely some misogyny and racism going on. All the more reason to have a fresh look at the material, I say.

Thanks for reading. I hope you had as good a time as I did writing.

Cameron Dokey is the author of nearly thirty young people's titles. Sort of like birthdays, she's stopped counting. Her other fairy tales include *The Storyteller's Daughter* and *Beauty Sleep*. Her most recent Simon Pulse release is the romantic comedy *How Not to Spend Your Senior Year*.

When she's not at her desk, you can find Cameron in the kitchen creating some carbohydrate the likes of which Dr. Atkins would definitely not approve, or out working in the garden. She lives in Seattle, Washington, with four cats and one husband.